FROM THE ASHES

FIRES OF REDEMPTION

D1366586

FROM THE ASHES
FIRES OF REDEMPTION

XEN

Previously released in September 2012 and has been enhanced with new material.

Entangled Publishing, LLC
2614 South Timberline Road
Suite 109
Fort Collins, CO 80525
Visit our website at www.entangledpublishing.com.

Select Otherworld is an imprint of Entangled Publishing, LLC.

Edited by Alethea Spiridon
Cover design by Les Solot
Cover art from Depositphotos

Manufactured in the United States of America

Second Edition January 2017

To my friends—too many to name.
Without your support, this book wouldn't exist.

Chapter One

I am not my father.

I tell myself that every day. I tell myself that now, as I press my eye to the microscope viewer and try to restrain the urge to pull a man's spine out through the back of his neck. One man in particular, who's currently watching me in the sterile silence of the lab, his nose sneering and thin. Langdon. Always Langdon, whose personality is the living embodiment of the lab's perpetual stink of chemicals, astringent cleaner, and mouse droppings. Every day I'm tempted to kill him. Leave him strewn on the floor in pieces, red staining the lab's endless white. Every day he gives me a thousand opportunities.

But I don't.

Because no matter how many people I hurt, no matter how many I kill, no matter how many nations I topple beneath the crushing fist of tyranny...

I am not my father.

I'm only his shadow.

My name is Tobias Rutherford, and I am the instrument of mankind's destruction.

To the human world, to my father, I have only one name: Spark. I suppose it's a fitting name for the son and second-in-command of the world's most feared villain: the Lord High General Infernus Blaze. Yeah. I know. Some name. If I had a choice, I'd call him Michael. *Dad* would work, too. *Dad* would be easier. But he prefers Blaze—and if he's the flame, I'm only a glimmering reflection of his glory.

After twenty-five years, I should be used to the sidekick role. I grew up trailing in my father's wake. When he conquered Cambodia, Malaysia, Thailand, Vietnam, I stood at his side. While he set loose his flame and burned them to the ground, I watched. In my earliest memories he stands wreathed in embers and hellish smoke, his eyes alight with rage and madness, while Bangkok crumbles around us and our home goes up like paper touched by a match, and all around the sparks flit like fireflies in a slow and strange dance.

I was nine.

Nine years old when I understood my purpose, and my place in this world.

The humans make villains of us, Spark. They fear us. They hate us.

Borders flaked to ash amidst the screams of the dying, uniting destroyed nations into the foundation of his empire. Those who lived, served. Those who refused, died.

Not much of a choice.

We will show them hatred. We will show them fear. We will give them the villains they crave.

Under his orders, I took Laos. The country fell at my feet. They called me a thunder god descended from the heavens in a chariot of lightning, yet my work was still *his* victory. It was always his victory.

Only then, my son, will we rule this world.

I thought I'd escape it if I left. I couldn't run forever, but I'd found a brief reprieve at graduate school in the States, studying for my master's in biogenetic science at UC Berkeley. I want to know what makes people like my father and me different. I want to know what's so very broken in the cells that even now swell into violet-dyed, strange neon art at the other end of my microscope's lens as I slip another slide onto the plate. I want to know if it's true that we're predisposed to go bad. That it's encoded in our genes, a hardwired mental disorder that gives rise to these powers. That there's no changing us. No treatment for our diseased minds. No variant to our deviant genetics that might offer hope for something different.

Sometimes I think there is no hope.

No hope for us to be anything but monsters.

They call us aberrants. Aberrant genetics. Aberrant psychology. We are sociopaths, psychopaths, sadists, freaks — a sickness of the worst kind, rejected by man and nature alike. We're the villains painted in every shocking role on television. Serial killers. School shooters. Pathological offenders. Yet as long as we're just fiction, we're the compelling rogues humans love to hate, painted with a certain form of pathos that minimizes our atrocities and allows us empathy. Make us real and we become less than human. Terrifying. Monstrous. Unworthy of empathy, unfit for psychological treatment, incurable. They fear our power, but our power isn't what's truly frightening.

It's us.

You know the old saying: power corrupts, and absolute power corrupts absolutely. It's not true. We corrupt the power. We use it to destroy, to wreak terrible punishment on the species that gave birth to us. It's no surprise the humans hate us.

I think, were I capable of feeling more than shallow echoes, I would hate myself.

No one here knows I'm an aberrant, at least. No one knows I hurt people, break people, kill people. Not even the other grad students have a clue that quiet, antisocial Tobias is Spark. Neither does Langdon.

Excuse me. *Doctor* Langdon. I've no idea how he landed the role of head research scientist in the biogenetics department, but he makes sure I never forget his seniority. Langdon is the only thing standing between me and my predoctoral qualification. Without his approval, no PhD candidacy—which is why I spend my evenings slaving in his lab, sorting slides and listening to him preach about curing the monstrosities of aberrant genetics.

He calls me his research assistant. I think he confuses "research assistant" with "indentured servant."

Yeah. Even here, I'm just a sidekick. I'd wonder if it was a racial thing, but frankly Langdon's just a prick.

Really, it would be so much easier if I killed him.

He's on the warpath today. He's gone from staring at me to pacing the lab, talking to himself in that high, weasely voice, his head bobbing on his thin neck like a stork hunting for frogs. He stares down at his own reflection, which grimaces up at him from the glossy, pale-gray tiles.

"I don't understand it. All the pieces are there, but the carrier continuously destabilizes after propagation and I—I—" He moans and drags his hand through his hair. A few strands come loose in his fingers. "I can't present this before the board. They'll laugh me out of the department and give the grant to that asshole Brady."

Without lifting my head from the fluorescence microscope, I murmur, "Maybe there's an unknown autoimmune element. It only takes one trigger to wipe out the carrier before it can deliver the payload."

His frigid stare practically peels the skin from the back of my head. He clucks his tongue. "If you have time to theorize, you have time to run the comparisons from last year's transgenic mouse trials."

"Already done." I slide off my stool, shrug out of my lab coat, strip my latex gloves, and drop them in the bin. "And I've run comparative analyses on today's slides."

When I brush my fingers over the tray of dated slides, I let slip a small burst of electrical current—not even an amp, barely enough to prickle my fingertips with a fleeting sizzle, invisible to the human eye...but enough to rupture the cell walls on the samples. It's easy this time, thanks to the conductive quartz slides used in ultraviolet fluorescence microscopy. Using fluorescent elements lets us track modified viral RNA, which acts as a carrier to insert corrective genes into the cells of transgenic mice modified with aberrant human DNA. The glass slides used in other tests are harder to tamper with, but I'll find a way. I always find a way. I don't want to be *corrected*.

I just want to understand.

"This batch looks like a bust," I say. "The carrier's too aggressive, and it's still propagating after cell penetration. The cells burst after first-stage replication."

"Thank you, Mr. Rutherford. I wasn't aware you were running this lab."

"Of course not, Doctor. I spoke out of turn. I'm sorry." I've mastered the ability to mask scathing sarcasm and violent homicidal urges behind polite deference, but sometimes I wonder how it flies over his head so easily. Restraining a sigh, I scoop up my backpack. "I'm late for my evening class."

Langdon flicks his spidery fingers at me. "Fine, whatever. Just get out."

I suppress my smile and, weaving through the rows of narrow tables and equipment, slip out of the lab. Even here I'm still doing my father's work, but in this case, I don't mind. I may not like being my father's shadow, but I'd never help a human exterminate my kind. We're born the way we are. We can't help it. There has to be some middle ground that will let us simply *live*, and if I can, I'll find it before people like Langdon unleash a "cure" that will kill us all.

My Bluetooth headset rings as I clatter down the stairs. I tap the switch on the edge. "Hi, Dad."

It's on my tongue to call him Blaze, and it tastes bitter. But I'm in public, and sound carries. The last thing I need is some pimply undergrad catching me talking to the leading contestant on *America's Next Top Psychotic Dictator*.

"Son."

His voice is deep, almost soothing. Maybe that's why aberrants flock to his cause. It's hard to imagine that voice as evil. He plays the benevolent shepherd too well, sheltering society's loathsome rejects in his love. Promising a safe haven where they can be free of human persecution. Vowing to give them the strength to fight for their rights. It's a good message, in theory. In reality, the execution is a bit bloodier and more despotic, but even I still buy into the cult sometimes. Too many memories, I guess.

When I was a kid, I thought that warmth was real.

"Any progress?" he asks.

"Minor sabotage. Langdon hasn't unearthed anything worrisome, but I'd rather keep him stalled."

"That's likely best. At the moment, though, I need to reposition you. While Langdon's research is a concern, I have better use for you elsewhere."

I stop at the foot of the steps, gripping the cool metal bar of the door. Through the slit of a window I can see the night outside, dark and defined by blue shadows. "Where?"

"New York. I'd like you to deal with a certain senator."

I glance over my shoulder. The stairwell is empty, but I drop my voice anyway. "If I assassinate a political figure, I'll be exposed. I thought the point was for me to stay in deep cover."

"The point," he says, his voice chilling, "is for you to be my presence in America, and to act on my behalf. I need you in New York. For as long as it takes. You can disable him without killing him and still maintain your cover."

"I can't transfer now. It's nearly the end of the semester. It'll look too suspicious, and there aren't any universities in New York with an equivalent to my degree program."

"Once you've finished your mission, you'll come back here. I don't see any point in remaining overseas for your education when we have perfectly competent scientific personnel here. You're old enough to be out of school and doing something with your life."

Of course. As long as that "something" is helping him dominate the world at large and never forgetting that my will is not my own; just an extension of his. I grit my teeth. "Is that an order, sir?"

"It is," he says flatly. "I'll have the necessary data sent to your email. Is your connection encrypted?"

"New algorithm every thirty seconds."

"I'll expect an update soon."

"Sure. You know me. Ever faithful."

"To—"

I can't listen to another word. With a sigh, my stomach heavy as a brick, I hang up, close my eyes, and lean against the door. It figures. The moment I get settled in and start making a life for myself, he uproots it for the sake of his grand plan. Not that "burn everything standing" is much of a plan.

Not that I have much of a life, either.

•••

I drive home to an empty apartment, an echoing and sterile space that looks like a show home for a jet-setting socialite. No roommate. No friends. No boyfriend. I don't even live on campus. I can't afford to let anyone too close. One casual slip, and it's over. My first year in the States, a lab assistant caught me using my abilities to interface with the campus intranet and access Dr. Langdon's personnel files, class schedule, and records of his grant applications. Hiding the corpse wasn't easy. Harder still was removing the fingerprints, and the teeth.

The face was already burned well beyond recognition. A hundred thousand volts at point-blank range will do that.

I've had to do the same to two others over the years. Kalen was the worst. Possibly because Kalen thought I loved him. That I was even capable of love. I'd met him through Debbie, who'd been my mentor in the biogenetics program. Nice girl. Had a girlfriend, Patricia or something. They'd been my friends, back when I thought I could still pretend to have friends. That having *friends* would help my cover, instead of just exposing me to greater risk that someone would realize what I am.

Kalen had been just a touch stupid, in a sweet way. Stupid enough to make for acceptable cover. But Debbie had been smart; smart enough to keep me on my toes in the lab. Smart enough to notice something was off.

Smart enough to start to figure me out.

I'd been dating Kalen for a few months by then. At first I didn't understand why he'd started acting strangely. Until the questions started. The kind of probing, analytical questions Kalen wouldn't think to ask. He was all puppy-dog eyes and that confused tilt of the head that came every time he didn't understand something. It didn't take long to figure out Debbie was behind the interrogation. Debbie suspected I might be an aberrant, and was using Kalen for information.

At that point, I'd had to get rid of them both.

Sleeping with a human had been a mistake, no matter how short-lived. Letting down my guard, though? Sheer idiocy. Naïveté.

You can be damned sure I wasn't that stupid when

disposing of the bodies.

I'd rather not have to do that again. It's more difficult to deal with when I don't have the mask, the identity of Spark, to hide behind. I don't like seeing their faces, instead of just a wave of bodies collapsing at my feet. It's hard not to remember the look in Kalen's eyes when I killed him in the same bed where we'd fucked the night before.

The day after, I'd felt like I should cry. Should miss him, with his weird little habits and the way he'd looked ten years old when his face lit up with that stupid smile. Should grieve the way Patricia had grieved, obsessively walking the campus and putting up signs with Debbie's soft brown face and a phone number below tall, blocky, accusing letters reading *HAVE YOU SEEN THIS WOMAN?* So much genuine emotion that I should have been able to reflect in some way. Any way.

Nothing.

Always, nothing.

I felt no remorse for anything. Not killing. Not hurting people. Not lying. Not the lie I'd told Langdon about my evening class, either. Ethics of Transgenic Animal Testing, taught by Professor Sean Archer, was officially canceled for the night. Something about Archer being sick. I'd overheard my classmates planning to fill in the hours with a San Francisco beach trip. I hadn't been invited. I hadn't expected to be. Even if people don't *know*, they never feel quite comfortable around me.

Yeah. I don't have much of a social life anymore.

Frankly, I'd rather be in class. The subject of ethics itself bores me: tedious human morality, people desperately grasping at anything to convince themselves they aren't animals. Instead, I spend the lectures listening to Archer without really hearing him. He's from Manchester, and that cultured British lilt to his otherwise rough, gravelly voice tends to hypnotize me. That voice shouldn't fit him so well. It's the voice of a large man, a dangerous man. Archer, while tall and broad-shouldered, is lean and bookish and almost too pretty.

The only thing dangerous about him is his eyes. They're sly, a green so pale it's almost white. Those eyes always find me the moment I've zoned out and lost track of the discussion topic. He's embarrassed me in class more times than I can count.

Maybe I should be glad class is canceled.

By the time I swap slacks for jeans and settle on the couch with my laptop, my email is already overflowing with messages from my father's aide, Jeremy. I open the files and skim through. Senator Rick Cranston, New York, landslide winner of the 2014 congressional election. So he just took office a few years ago; interesting. If he's made himself a threat already, he's probably young. Ambitious. Arrogant.

I like arrogant. Arrogant men are easier to kill. They make more blind mistakes, confident they won't fail.

Someone's compiled a book's worth of information on the senator's daily routine, hobbies, voting history, even a few things the press would pay millions to know. It would be easier if I could just turn him over to TMZ and let the vultures do the dirty work for me, but Dad's out for blood. Ruining Cranston's career wouldn't do anything but give him enough free time and enough of a vendetta to do even more damage than he's already done.

There are photos, too. Healthy tan, full head of hair, surgically perfect smile. Dad must have an informant to get all this. Too bad he doesn't have his informants do the dirty work, especially if they're human. With my style of wetwork, there's usually no doubt an aberrant was involved. There'll be a media firestorm. Fearmongering. Retaliation.

But that's probably what Dad wants. Fuel for his fire.

The last file is the most incriminating. New legislation on aberrants that proposes stripping us of our rights and treating us as illegal aliens. The bill includes huge budget grants to turn Federal Immigration and Naturalization Services into an anti-aberrant military task force capable of containing us and expelling us from the country.

Typical. Kill it, or make it someone else's problem.

There's even an outline for a research facility. The words "Quarantine Zone" and "Treatment Center" practically vibrate off the page.

Quarantine. Treatment. Lock us up. Sedate us into helplessness. Experiment. Cure us. Make us normative. Or if that's impossible, imprison us and use us. Manipulate our genes for their own benefit. Aberrants are just the new transgenic mice.

But if we're mice, then the ones holding the keys to our cages are rats through and through.

I set the laptop on the coffee table. The *clink* against the glass brings Samadhi running from the bedroom; she always thinks it's her food dish. She's big even for a Maine Coon, a silver tabby cream puff, and she waddles when she walks. With a mewl, she noses my foot, struggles up onto the couch, and makes herself very uncomfortable in my lap. Grunting, I shift her until I can breathe, then run my fingers through her fur.

"Well, my tubby little Buddha," I murmur. "Looks like I'm going to New York."

I'm not moving, or transferring schools. Dad can go to hell. Semester break is coming soon. Christmas, the busiest travel season of the year. It won't seem strange if I take a vacation over break.

It won't even be hard to travel under a false identity. Dad has front corporations on top of front corporations scattered throughout the country. His fingers are in everything. If he can turn his Thailand-born son into a third-generation Thai American citizen with family in Georgia, he can turn me into a foreign tourist long enough to fly to New York, assassinate a senator, and fly back to California.

Samadhi sticks her damp nose into my cheek. I scratch under her chin. "At least I know someone loves me, as long as I feed you."

It's too bad she can't talk back. There's never anyone to talk back. This apartment is too big for one person; too big for just me and one oversize cat. It's too quiet, too dark, yet filled with the whispers of a thousand secrets I can never tell. They're in every corner, every shadow. A murder here. A massacre there. The enslavement of an entire country, and worse. Worse in my past, and worse to come. Things I can't erase. Things I can't turn back from. Even if I let myself feel for the people who've suffered because of me, because of *him*, all the guilt in the world won't undo what's already been done. Guilt is a self-indulgent emotion, anyway. Not something I deserve.

I am not my father, but I am indeed my father's son—and we are villains in a world without heroes.

I need to get away. Away from the apartment; away from its secrets; away from these reflections I shouldn't be bothered by, yet can't stand to see. It's too bad I can't get away from myself. Too bad I can't truly be the son my father wants me to be, and turn my back on the human race. Life would be easier if I didn't wonder. If I didn't think, sometimes…

Maybe we were meant for something more.

The whispers follow me as I slip on a button-down shirt and boots, grab my coat and car keys, and head out into the night.

Chapter Two

It's cold outside, colder than when I came home. California is supposed to be warm, even in winter, but I'm used to heat and rain. Thailand never quite had winter, even before it disappeared into the new nation of Xinth, its sprawling cities and temples and straw villages swallowed into the faceless walls of uniform steel in my father's preplanned empire. Xinth or Thailand, the weather never changed. There was only summer, the rains, and the cool season, which rarely dropped below pleasantly sunny. Most Northern Californians call their mid-fifties December weather "mild."

I'm freezing my narrow brown ass off.

I have no idea what possessed me to drive to Memorial Stadium. With the lights dark, the football team and fans and television crews gone, it's like a dream. Hollow. Silent in that special way dreams are silent, an empty stillness that exists only in the most deserted of places.

The wind is strongest in the upper levels of the stands, hitting me with a cold slap that smells faintly of the bay. I settle near the press box, letting the wall shelter me from the strongest gusts, and huddle into my jacket. I don't know what I'm doing here. This isn't a place for people like me. It's a place for people to be together, to share in something greater than themselves. By night there's nothing left but the lingering scents of mustard and sweat and cut grass, and the imaginary echoes of excited tension, victory, defeat.

I've never been to any of the games, though some of the players are in my elective classes. Right now they're out on the beach, laughing at things that are only funny when you're drunk, complaining about the sand and the cold, doing things they'll regret when it's time to roll out of bed for practice and fill this stadium with life. I don't belong with them. They don't even know my name. That's the way it's meant to be.

I can't ever forget that.

It takes me a while to realize there's someone else here. He leans against the wall ringing the field far below, looking out over the perfect green synthetic turf. His casual posture and lithe build are familiar, but I can't quite make him out from up here. He turns his head. Long black hair sweeps over his shoulders, and I glimpse his delicate profile, the gleam of narrow rimless glasses.

Dr. Archer.

He doesn't look sick; his skin is pale, but that's normal, a sort of soft moonstone whiteness that looks almost translucent. His shirt is rumpled, untucked, half-unbuttoned, his jeans loose and low-slung, his hair tousled and windswept. He's almost a different person, in the darkness of the night. In class his shirts and slacks are always perfect, every hair smoothed neatly into a tail, nothing out of place. Prim. Proper. Upright.

Not the man standing below.

He lifts a cigarette to his lips, then exhales a thin cloud of white. I had no idea he even smoked, but he's really not the kind of professor to fraternize with his students in his off hours. I've never even been to see him during his office hours. When I keep my distance, I do it with a vengeance. And Archer isn't someone who's ever really been on my radar as anything other than a pretty distraction, saying words that mean nothing to me for one hour a night, three nights a week.

I draw my jacket closer, fingers clenching in the soft leather. I can barely see his face from this high, but something in the set of his shoulders, the way he holds himself, says there's something wrong. I should go before he sees me.

I rise and edge down the stands, placing my feet silently. My father trained me to move without being seen. Sometimes that means stealth, but more often it means blending in. In a crowd of ordinary people, the one moving with the purpose and grace of a lifelong fighter stands out; in the patterns of self-absorption created by each person forging ahead on the paths of their own lives, it's the one who's watching what everyone else is doing who draws suspicion. On campus, I've cultivated the aimless, absent stride of an academic. In New York, it'll be the distracted wandering of a tourist. People remember body language before faces, recognize it at an innate animal level. It says who you are, how you see yourself.

Change that, and you can walk right past someone without being recognized.

Right now, Archer's body language is setting off warning bells. Halfway down the stands I pause, trying to figure out what's making me uncomfortable, trying to understand this ineffable sense of melancholy.

That's my mistake.

If I'd kept walking, he'd probably have ignored me as background noise. It's the pause that stands out, that makes him turn his head. Those green eyes lance into me, shadowed beneath sharply arched brows. I jerk. For an instant, I'm in the lecture hall, and he's asking me about the Pruitt sentience debates on the boundary between transgenic organisms and humans—when I haven't looked at a single slide in the last hour's presentation.

Recognition flickers across his face. His weary smile eases that skewering look. "Mr. Rutherford. It appears I've been caught."

There's no help for it now. Pushing my hands into my pockets, I descend to ground level and halt a casual distance away. "I doubt anyone cares, Dr. Archer."

"Please—we're not in class. It's Sean."

He flicks ash from his cigarette. From the scent, it's a clove. Its exotic, spicy musk is sweeter than the sour stench of regular cigarettes. I've caught a whiff now and then when turning in papers at his desk, but hadn't been able to place it until now. I don't like smokers—their teeth, the lingering odor, their rasp—but he smells good.

Forbidden fruit always does.

"What are you doing out here, Sean?" I try out his name, tasting it on a sigh.

"I like it out here." Sean's eyes half-close as he takes another drag off the cigarette. "It's nothing but after-impressions. Ghosts replacing the overpowering crush and clamor. Quiet in a place that's meant to be loud."

"You like contradictions." I lean against the wall at his side. I barely reach above his shoulder. He's tall, even for an Englishman, while I take after my mother's spare, compact build.

"Trying to analyze me, young Mr. Rutherford?"

Young. I snort. Sean's only thirty-two, seven years my senior. "Just observing."

"That would be a first." Shifting to face me, he studies me with a dry quirk of his lips. "I'm starting to think you don't like my class. Or you're catching up on your beauty sleep."

I shrug. "You teach ethics. It's a pointless subject."

"I'm wounded." Yet he laughs, albeit cynical and brief. "Go on then. Enlighten me."

But I hold my tongue, watch him, wonder. Wonder how honest I can be. Yet if he is not himself tonight, not the Dr. Archer I know, then perhaps I am not the Tobias I pretend to be, either.

And perhaps in this shadowed ghost-land filled with the memories of the daytime world, I can be honest.

"There's nothing to enlighten," I say. "Humans are animals. You can't teach them to be something they're not. The entire concept of morals and ethics is a subjective game of pretend, one based entirely in human prejudice. Bias. People say 'I don't like that' and try to turn an unreasoned preference into a universal law, when there are no universal laws. To think otherwise is futile. It's asking for disappointment, to think we're all preprogrammed with some established set of higher rules."

"So you prefer to live without morals?"

"I prefer to live without being forced to follow someone else's moral code."

"And you think that would make the world a better place."

"I think it would make it a less judgmental place, if we eliminate these concepts of good or bad, better or worse. If we accept that our hatred for what we call 'evil' isn't about some immutable concept of evil, but about our own fear."

The words come by rote. Textbook philosophy, regurgitated nihilism, spouting off wordy academic ideals like it's nothing but theory and not something killing people like me every day. It's almost surreal, to stand here talking about this as high-handed, pompous talking points when I've seen exactly what humans will do to us if they succeed in locking us away for being *evil*.

But I can't say that. All I can do is ramble on like your typical grad student, high on his illusions of intellectual superiority.

Sean only looks at me, his eyes hooded and thoughtful, a smile teasing the arches and dips of his mouth. The cold flushes his lips a dusky red. Those lips make me want to do things. Things that make my gut turn hot and tight. Things that force me to look away. Still he says nothing, and I frown.

"What?"

"Nothing." He shakes his head. "You simply sound a great deal like my younger brother. He used to be fascinated by these...aberrants, is that what they're called? Thought of them as comic book villains. These poor, tragic antiheroes, doomed to a terrible fate."

"Aberrants are nothing but monsters."

"Are they? I wonder." He takes another drag off his clove and turns that penetrating gaze away from me, giving me room to breathe. "We call them monsters, but what if they're only monsters because they're made that way?"

My fists clench in my pockets. "They're born that way. You can't change genetics."

"But you can change behavior, Mr. Rutherford. What we are at the genetic level doesn't change that we have the right to choose *who* we are, whether we choose to be human... or choose to be monsters. Someone born with a congenital disease still chooses to be a good or bad person, and that has nothing to do with their disease. Someone born homosexual can be a saint or a sinner, but the genetics that make them homosexual are neutral. To say otherwise is to deny the richness and complexity of the human experience. Science is neutral. It's only humans who impose value judgments on it."

His tone is light, almost mocking, but there's a faint flash of challenge in his eyes, kindling an answering spark. I want to tell him the truth. I want to open his blind, innocent eyes and show him the ugliness of the world. I want to show him the ugliness inside *me*.

I want to hurt him.

I want to know how his voice sounds, rising in gasps of pain. I want to see red streaked over that pretty white skin, trailing in rivulets as if his veins were painted on the outside. I want to see his eyes go stark with fear, then dull, then dark, then empty. I want to feel that tingle, that shiver, that surging high as rolling waves of electricity pour from my body into his, while he arches and screams.

But more than anything, I want to kiss the naïveté right out of him. Kiss him until his lips bruise and bleed and he melts against me.

And that's one thing I cannot do.

If he knew what I was, if he knew the *thoughts* pouring through my mind in a scarlet torrent, his morals would conveniently change. He would make a choice, all right. He'd choose to see me as something other than human, all because of one strand of DNA.

I can't do anything. I can't say anything. All I can do is smile in that tight, withdrawn way that so perfectly fits a poorly socialized science major. I don't know how to smile any other way when it's the only shield protecting Sean from the way my fingers ache to reach for him. It's gut-deep. Visceral. It's the only thing I know how to feel with any true intensity, and right now it's dangerous for that intensity to fix on him.

Yet I keep my voice as neutral as possible when I speak. I have a lifetime of practice at this, painting over my ugliness to leave the blandness of social acceptability. "You must be used to living in perpetual disappointment."

"Perpetual disappointment," he repeats thoughtfully. He says nothing else for long moments, his eyes narrowed, his lips pursed. "What a lonely life you must lead. Never have faith in anyone, and they can never disappoint you."

That hits hard, a ten-ton punch that guts me, shoves my heart up against the ropes. My face feels like wax, frozen in place as I struggle not to betray the sick feeling rising up in my throat. "Analyzing me, now?"

"Perhaps. I only wonder…if you had to decide, in a split

second, whether to take the right path or the one of self-preservation, what would you do?"

"You know the answer to that."

"Maybe. Maybe I don't. I think, were you ever in that situation, you might change your mind."

"Then let's hope I'm never in that situation." I have to change the subject. It's too personal and makes me too angry. I can't risk that. "Why did you cancel class if you aren't sick?"

He flinches. He really is rather pretty, in a brooding, thoughtful way, especially when his lashes sweep downward and he turns away. I catch myself wondering how his skin feels, if it's as smooth as it looks. If it's as fragile as it looks, and how easily he could break. I have to force myself to focus when he speaks again.

"I had plans for tonight. They fell through. It happens."

There's a hitch to his voice, sullying its richness. Loss, I think. Maybe even heartbreak. It's hard to tell. I've never been very good with human emotions. I understand their violence, their pettiness, their cruelty, their lusts—all the things humans and aberrants share. Yet they have so many more passions, these creatures of whims and changing moods. Sorrow. Love. Joy. Empathy. Tenderness. All delicate things, too delicate for me to handle without crushing.

"So she stood you up." When he winces, I don't know if I enjoy it or hate it. My father has this driving need to destroy anything beautiful. It's an obsession, maybe one I share. Aberrant genetics. Deviant mind. Deviant pleasures, dark and cruel and hungry.

"Something like that," he says.

"I'm sorry for prying."

"It's fine. I must look a fright, out here moping because yet another man has walked out on me." His laugh is as bitter and rich as dark coffee. "You'd think I'd be used to it by now. Enough not to act like a child about it."

Another man. I don't need to know that. It sends my thoughts back where they don't belong. "Getting dumped hurts. I think you're allowed to mope for a bit."

"Hardly appropriate in front of a student."

"Like you said, we're not in class."

Sean looks at me sidelong and laughs. It's sweeter this time, the sound melting down my spine and curling, silky and warm, in my gut. "You're a bloody idiot, Tobias—may I call you Tobias?"

"Sure." Inside my chest, something tightens at the way he says my name, rolling it across his lips. Gods, that mouth. It keeps drawing me back, enthralling me. "So what happened?"

"The same thing that always happens." He stubs his clove out on the wall, grinding a black smear into the white paint. Propping his chin in his hand, he glances over the empty stands. "He wanted to take things further. My head said yes. My mouth said no. He left."

"Your head says yes, your mouth says no... What does your heart say?"

He stills and looks at me strangely. "I don't know. Odd. I don't think I ever go into these relationships thinking about my heart."

"I thought that's what a relationship was supposed to be about."

"You say that as if you don't know."

I deflect with a shrug and a half smile. "I'm a lab tech. My particular genus isn't known for its long dating history."

"I don't believe you."

"Why not?"

"I just don't. Your lips say one thing, but..." He searches my face, as if he can see through me. As if he knows everything. "You have the darkest eyes. There's nothing there. Nothing at all. It's like you don't exist."

"My eyes are black. You couldn't see anything if you tried."

"I am trying," he says. "Has no one ever done so before?"

I can't answer that. I don't know how. I can only look at him. My lips part, but no words come out. He draws closer, looking down at me as if he can see all my secrets—no. As if he can see my *worst* secret, my deepest shame.

As if he can see how weak I am, how unfit to carry the weight of this double life.

"You're so angry," he says softly. "At what? At me?"

I clench my jaw and lower my eyes. "No."

"Then what?"

The touch of his fingertips to my cheek kindles the electricity in my veins, until the fine hairs on my arms stand on end. I flinch.

"Don't. Don't touch me."

His hand falls away. "You claim to hate aberrants so much, yet you seem determined to live like them. Without morals. Without emotions. If you admire them enough to mimic them, why do you hate them so?"

I can't stay here. I can't be near him. The more he pries at me, the more he *looks* at me, the more I fear I'll do something I'll regret. I take a few steps back and force myself to look at him. He's so warm. I can't do this. I can't want that warmth, can't deal with the tightness in my chest when I realize how much he's hurting. How much he needs someone right now. Anyone.

No. He's my professor. He's human. He's a blind, idealistic fool, and it makes him beautiful and strange and entirely compelling.

And I can't ever be that stupid again.

Yet he's still waiting for me to speak, still waiting for my answer and watching me with those patient, expectant eyes. Asking me *why*. Asking me to tell him the truth, when the only way I know how to survive is to lie.

"Because an aberrant killed my mother," I say, and walk away.

Chapter Three

Maybe if I tell myself I'm not running, I'll actually believe it.

His voice chases me, calling my name, but I won't look back. I shut myself in my car, but rather than start the engine I slam my forehead against the steering wheel and laugh—this hollow, cracking thing that feels like it's crumbling my ribs. I'm a fool. I shouldn't have told him that. I've never told *anyone* that. I've never had to. Everyone in Xinth knows what happened to my mother. In their eyes, she deserved it. She'd tried to take me away from my father. Tried to raise me as human. Of course he'd had to kill her and reclaim what was his.

Of course.

My phone rings again. Bad timing. My throat is tight, and I doubt I'll be able to hide the choke in my voice. I don't want to talk to anyone, but I have no choice unless I want to answer uncomfortable questions about where I was. Caller ID says it's Jeremy. The lesser of a dozen evils, at least. I tap my headset and try to get my voice under control.

"What is it now?"

"Young Master." He always calls me that, though he's only a year older. Ever the faithful retainer to the royal family, as long as it benefits him.

He's an overblown secretary.

The encryption delay makes his voice crackle. "Was it really wise to argue with him, Tobias?"

My upper lip curls. "Did he kill anyone?"

"I've handled it," he answers neutrally. "Nothing burned." A pause. "I'm afraid this isn't a social call. There's been a change of plans."

"New York?"

"Not anymore." I hear tapping on the other end of the line. Jeremy types like he has a grudge against the keyboard. "New Hampshire. The senator has a lake house there, and his itinerary shows he'll be there for New Year's. Alone."

"That's three weeks from now. I can't plan an assassination in three weeks."

"You have a plan this time? Last I checked, your modus operandi involved fire and screaming."

"Don't confuse me with my father." I scowl. In the rearview mirror, my reflection scowls back. "This might have worked in New York. In a public place, where it's easy to make it look like an accident. In his home—"

"We minimize risk this way."

"My father doesn't trust me to handle it?"

A pregnant silence, then, "It's been some time, Tobias."

I see. So this isn't just a power play. It's a test. I've been away from the fold too long and have to prove I'm still loyal, even without my father here to grind me under his thumb. "Fine."

"You understand your mission then?"

My fingers curl against the steering wheel. I wish it were Jeremy's neck. "I do."

He chuckles coldly. "So *petulant* when you're angry. I look forward to your return home, young Master."

The line goes dead. I sigh. Home. That place isn't home, any more than this one. The only home I ever had burned to the ground.

Three weeks. With Langdon's grant presentation, homework, finals, and two fifty-page term theses, that's not much time. I'll need travel schedules. Blueprints of the lake house. Time to scout the place and plan my course of action. I'll have to leave right after finals.

I'm still sitting in the parking lot, just staring out at the night. Staring at nothing. When I uncurl my fingers from the steering wheel my knuckles creak, ache. I can't help looking in my side-view mirror, hoping to see Sean as I back out of the lot and turn toward home — but there's nothing.

That's the way it should be.

Yet I don't sleep well that night. Sean Archer haunts me.

I think, if you were ever in that situation, you might change your mind.

Would I? I've always known my path. Maybe it isn't what humans consider right, but it's the only path I have. Fight. Conquer. Kill...or be exterminated. I've never had to wonder, never had to question if there was any other way. My father defined my destiny before my birth. He will create his empire — and when he passes, I will rule in his stead.

Yet as I lay in bed, staring at the ceiling, I see only those pretty red lips asking a question I can never answer.

• • •

Saturday morning. My breakfast is burned. So are the edges of the blueprints I'm reading. I don't get along with certain electronic devices. I can mostly control the natural current in my body, but some electronics form a closed circuit loop on contact. Things short out. There's a reason I don't own a stereo system, and my laptop has been specially ruggedized and insulated. My iPod has fried and come back to life so many times I think it's a zombie. I'd thought the electric stove was on my safe list, until a shower of sparks burned holes in my printouts and turned my eggs over easy into eggs flambé.

The food tastes like shit. I eat it anyway. It's either that or Samadhi's kibble, and I don't feel like getting dressed and going out for groceries. I get little enough time to myself on weekends as it is. Langdon wants me in the lab this afternoon, leaving only a few hours to focus on my real work.

Burned eggs aren't the best brain food. I'm coming up empty. Staging a heart attack is out of the question. The senator's a vegan, in peak physical condition, with no known or hereditary heart conditions. The patio hot tub looks promising. One electrocuted corpse taking a swim with a shorted household appliance, no autopsy required. That might actually work, if it wasn't December. Too cold for the senator to be taking a dip outdoors with the toaster oven. Even if I frame it as a suicide, it's suspect. The plumbing schematics indicate indoor whirlpool tubs, but that would require breaking and entering—without leaving any evidence or running afoul of the household staff. Too complicated.

The more complicated the plan, the more likely it is to fuck up.

A lightning strike would be quick, something I could manage from a distance, but too conspicuous. I don't even know why I'm trying *not* to be conspicuous when sooner or later my father will claim credit anyway, just to incite panic. It's just my way. I prefer to do things quietly, keep to myself. Save the theatrics for someone else. The quieter I am, the easier it is to just *live* in the lulls between the storms.

Screw it. I'll scope out the house when I get there. In the cold. I hear there's snow in New Hampshire. I'm looking forward to it. Really.

I take my breakfast and blueprints to the couch, flip on CNN, and listen for any news that might affect my travel plans. I sent my itinerary to Jeremy last night. He'll arrange for my tickets, my fake ID, and any cover I might need—and handle the fallout when my father realizes it's a round-trip ticket. In. Out. Back to Berkeley. Back to the life I've made for myself. Strange and isolated it may be, but it's still *mine*.

I'll probably get a blistering phone call later. It'll be worse for Jeremy. I should feel bad for that. I don't. Maybe that makes me an asshole, but I'm not ready for that final showdown yet. Not until I have something concrete to back me up. Not until I'm sure I can stand on my own once I cut loose and find my own place in the world.

Not until I'm sure there's even a place for me.

It flits through my head in something close to a whisper. I never let myself think it out loud. If I think it out loud, I have to acknowledge that maybe, just maybe, there's something seditious brewing inside me. Something dangerous. Something I don't know how to deal with, when acting on it could bring hell down on my head.

The newscaster's voice catches my attention. I set the blueprints down, pick up the remote, and turn up the volume.

"—local authorities have raised the Bay Area terror threat level to yellow—"

Threat levels. Gods, those piss me off. Humans so afraid of anything *not like them* that they'll gun their own kind down in the street, then declare *threat level yellow has been neutralized, victory is ours* because they succeeded in destroying anything *not like them*.

It's a miracle they haven't exterminated themselves by now. Fighting to the death over skin color and gender and religion. Abusing police power to murder innocents. Even worse, the passive neutrality that turns every death into nothing but another story on the news, watched with little interest before going back to their iPhones and their lattes and their lives as long as they remain personally unaffected. They know we walk among them. They know we hide in plain sight. But it only matters to them when they're directly in danger; when they have an *other* to point to and say, *I'm afraid, I'm afraid, they're different, and I'm afraid.*

Until then, it's not real. Just someone else's problem that they don't have to care about.

And they call us monsters.

"—increased security at San Francisco International Airport after a failed hijacking by an aberrant terrorist group claiming to be from the rebel nation of Xinth," the broadcast continued. "The hijacking attempt, which occurred at 3:42 a.m., ended in catastrophe when a hijacker lost control of his powers and the plane was unable to take off. In the ensuing chaos, police and military counterterrorism forces were able to subdue and imprison these menaces to public safety. The Xinthian dictator has yet to make a public statement claiming responsibility for these actions, and satellite surveillance remains unable to penetrate the barrier surrounding the aberrant stronghold."

The barrier. That's Jeremy's real job, not managing my father's day planner. He's able to affect the physical state of matter at the fundamental level, and he's transmuted simple air into a barrier solid enough to repel nuclear weapons, yet malleable enough to allow our people to slip in and out at his discretion. The wave-scrambling signal permeating the barrier is my work. We use coded wireless signals that change frequencies and encryption at randomized intervals, controlled by a programmed algorithm. The same algorithm controls the scrambling signal, changing it at matching intervals to allow only our transmissions through. Without the barrier and that signal, Xinth—officially the Unitary State of Xinthphlam, the Thai word for "phoenix"—would have been nuked into the ground ages ago.

My father may have the most idiotic name in the history of villainy, but he's still a brilliant tactician.

Which is why this terrorist attack doesn't make sense. It isn't his style. He likes to make flamboyant statements and declarations of war against our human oppressors, but the real work goes on behind the scenes while his grandstanding distracts the world at large.

The mill of God grinds slow, but it grinds exceeding fine, he's fond of saying. I suppose he fancies himself to be his God, taking his time placing each element of his plans into place and only executing when the moment is perfectly right. He doesn't work on small scales like plane hijackings. He's more likely to torch an entire subcontinent, and he'd never send anyone so incompetent they can't control their own powers. It just doesn't fit.

And I need to stop obsessing over it. It's probably just some splinter group hoping to claim Xinth's protection. I'll ask Dad about it after he's done tearing me a new one.

After trashing the eggs, I feed Samadhi, shower, dress, and head for the lab. I'm early, but I like it that way. It gives me time to investigate Langdon's files for anything useful and gives me a few hours of peace without his complaining.

Settling at Langdon's workstation, I fire up his PC and press my palm to the tower. Most don't think about the fact that everything a computer does, even a single key press, requires an electronic signal that, in the end, boils down to flipping a switch between one and zero. A typed password is just several electronic signals, ones and zeros lining up until they mean something useful. Another signal initiates password authentications, and still another lets the computer log on. With a little concentration and finesse I can bypass everything and, with minor electrical pulses at nearly the atomic level, flip those switches, toggling between one and zero to fool the computer into thinking it's authenticated a successful log-on.

On unfamiliar computers it can take me hours to figure out their components and the encryption embedded in their operating systems, but I've been spoofing Langdon's PC for so long I have it unlocked in minutes. His desktop background is a picture of an anime catgirl with ludicrously large breasts. Again. Last time there were tentacles involved. The keys feel sticky. I'll be nuking my hands with Purell after this.

Nothing interesting on his desktop. I lose myself for wasted hours browsing through smug, self-satisfied annotations in the sample tracking database, then check his voice logs. Langdon uses a digital recorder during work then copies the files to his desktop. There's a new one from last night. I peer past the monitor to make sure the lab is empty and the door is closed, then drop the file into the media player. That voice I've learned to hate pipes from the speakers, tinny and nasal.

"Reviewing results of lab trial 426-B. There's an anomaly I'm not seeing. I've observed real-time carrier insertion and replication from beginning to end. It looks promising. The carrier properly targets aberrant genome sequence PQH-X. The corrective gene therapy should work, but the slides all show massive deterioration. How? The cell-wall ruptures indicate typical viral replication, but the absence of new viral material is a conundrum. There must be an external factor. Beginning trial 427-A tomorrow, using a modified viral carrier with limited reproductive faculties. This has to work. I'm tired of this. I need this grant. This problem can't stop me."

The recording ends. I swear under my breath. Langdon's catching on. He tends to be sloppy about checking slides and leaves that to me. I'd hoped he wouldn't notice the anomaly; while the ruptures in the cell walls are normal, usually that rupture is caused by newly spawned viral RNA bursting free to spread and infect other cells. But when that rupture is caused by a meddling electromaniac? The absence of viral replication is noticeable — if you have the sense to know what you're looking for. I don't really trust Langdon's sense, but I shouldn't have underestimated his anal-retentiveness or obsession with making a name for himself as the first human to create an aberrant cure.

I'll have to either find a more subtle way to tamper with the samples, or eliminate him entirely. I can't let him find his cure. I'm not a problem to be solved, and to hell with the good of the human race. I want to survive. No one can tell me that's wrong.

"Tobias?"

I jump. A surreptitious click closes the open folders. Sean leans through the lab door.

I peer at him over the top of the monitor. He's in casual dress today, and *still* doesn't look a thing like my straight-laced professor. He looks like a punk-rock prince plucked right out of a grungy London underground club. Frayed, ripped jeans cling to his narrow hips, barely weighted in place by several slim leather belts crisscrossed over denim. Biker boots. Leather wristbands. A sleeveless Depeche Mode shirt, loose enough to fall off one sleek, smoothly toned shoulder. Black nail polish. A tangle of pewter pendants on leather cords, dangling against the fine line of his clavicle.

Well. This is a new side to Sean Archer.

I must have the damnedest look on my face, because he looks uncomfortable, even embarrassed. He tucks his wild hair behind his ear. "Sorry, are you busy?"

"Ah. No. Just looking at some research notes." I lock the computer and stand. "Are you looking for Dr. Langdon?"

"You, actually. With the fits Langdon's been throwing lately, I thought you might be in. You should have seen him last night — "

He closes his mouth abruptly. I frown. What was Sean

doing with Langdon last night?

"Late-night faculty meeting?" I ask blandly.

"Something like that." He clears his throat. "Look, about last night…"

"It's fine. I never saw you."

"It's not that."

I blink and he smiles, his composure returning with a low laugh.

"Though I suppose it should be," he continues. "Fraternizing with a student. I should be ashamed." With a self-deprecating twist of his lips, he shrugs. "Still. I wanted to thank you. I needed the company last night, even if I was too busy feeling sorry for myself to admit it. And, as confrontational and morally reprehensible as you may be, you made surprisingly good company."

I give him a flat look. "You're too kind."

"I'm teasing. I'm dreadfully awkward at this, really. Don't get out much, you know." He taps his lower lip with a fingertip, drawing my gaze to linger on the soft curve. "I should probably make some effort to change that. Since I owe you, what say I treat you to lunch?"

It takes me a moment to realize what the hot feeling creeping over my face is. I'm blushing. I don't think I've ever blushed in my life. "You don't owe me anything, really."

"I feel like I do. I seem to have blundered into some rather uncomfortable topics."

Yeah. So have I. Like wondering what the hell his involvement with Langdon is, and if all his talk about changing behavior was just a more PC version of Langdon's anti-aberrant spiel. There are some people like that out there. People who think if they just educate us on their moral superiority, they'll make aberrants less *aberrant* and more acceptable to their version of human society. *Narakas* forbid Sean be one of them: well intentioned, but ultimately clueless and hurtful.

Dammit. I need to focus on Cranston, not on Langdon's loose ends. If Sean turns out to be a problem, he'll have to be dealt with before I leave. So what if he's nice. So what if he's beautiful. It doesn't matter.

If he's a threat, he has to be eliminated.

Yet when he glances at me through those dark lashes, long wisps curving over pale eyes like a black widow's legs curling toward its prey, I'm on the verge of surrender. I'm not accustomed to being the prey, but I have the feeling I'm already snared.

"Really, Tobias," he says. "You'd think you'd relish the opportunity to tell me what else is wrong with my lessons. Besides, if you come, I'll tell you a secret."

"What's that?"

"The horrible things I did to my ex's belongings."

I groan. A smile twitches at my lips, one that feels strangely genuine. "You're just going to keep badgering me until I say yes, aren't you?"

"Indeed." He tilts his head with a charming, sly little smile, and I sigh.

"Let me get my coat."

I push my chair back and stand, and he smiles so sweetly for a moment I think his skin must be sugar, begging for a taste. Then it's gone, and he offers me his arm, green eyes glittering invitingly. I shouldn't take it. I do anyway, my hand curling in the crook of his elbow, his warmth as much of a shock to my skin as the first hot buzz of my electricity.

Gods. I don't know what the hell I'm doing, but I am so, so screwed.

Chapter Four

"Bleach," Sean says, his face alight with laughter. "All over Matt's Armani suits."

I don't want to laugh in the packed restaurant, as if there's something wrong with people *seeing* me express human emotion, but I can't help myself. We're at Le Petit Cheval, a French Vietnamese restaurant near campus. I don't get to eat Vietnamese often and was surprised when Sean let me pick. Le Petit Cheval is far enough from the school that I doubt anyone will see us together in the lunch rush crowd, which fills the small, dim restaurant from wall to wood-paneled wall.

Not that there's anything to see. I'm almost disappointed. Even though we left the lab arm in arm, there's been no contact since then. If I'm going to be accused of flirting with professors to boost my grades, I'd at least like there to be some actual flirting involved. I've done it in the past, to get information out of people without leaving a trail of bodies — or some approximation of flirting at least. In truth, I'm horrible at social byplay. Banter. Seduction. I manage, sometimes, by just being myself when for some, cruelty and seduction are the same thing.

And cruelty, I can do far too well.

"You don't seem like the vindictive type," I say.

Sean slides me a veiled look over the rims of his glasses. "What's my type, then?"

"Cool. Cultured. Reserved. A little terrifying."

"Terrifying?"

"Terrifying."

"Mm." He favors me with a chilly smile, and Dr. Archer's back. "Mr. Rutherford, please explain the significance of the 2013 Transgenic Experimentation Act."

I point my paper-wrapped chopsticks at him. "That."

He laughs. "How droll." He runs one slick black fingernail along the rim of his water glass. "I'll tell you a secret, if you promise not to spill a word of it."

"That would be the second secret. You seem fond of those."

"And contradictions." His fingernail strikes the glass with a little *tink*. "I grew up on a little cottage farm in Clovelly. The village is so small the donkeys outnumber the people, or they did. It's a tourist trap now. I didn't even learn to speak proper Queen's English until I went to university at Manchester, and that was just so the chavs would stop calling me Welshie."

"You're just giving me ammunition, Farmer Archer."

"Do you want to hear the secret or not?"

Do I? What if he tells me he's been working with Langdon? I feign a smile and bow my head. "Forgive me... farm boy."

"You're impossible. You're lucky I like you enough to tell you." He props his chin in his hand. "The thing is...every time I stand up in that lecture hall, I'm terrified. I revert back to that uncultured farm boy, with my backwoods twang and simple airs. Half my students are older than I, and I have no idea how to make them respect me. The only thing I can do is make them as afraid of me as I am of them."

"There's a flaw in your plan."

He raises a brow. "Oh? Do tell."

"You told me, and now those evil looks will never work on me again."

"Pity. I do so enjoy that vacant stare when I wake you." Sean sighs. "Really, is my class so dull?"

The waitress saves me from answering. I'd ordered *bun bo nuong*, cold rice noodles with beef kabobs. Sean has never eaten Vietnamese before, so he let me order for him: *bun ga nuong*, the same as mine but with chicken. Once she sets out cold glasses of lemon honey tea, the waitress excuses herself. Sean watches me expectantly, ignoring his food.

Persistent, isn't he.

I relent. "Your class isn't dull. It's just not something I believe in."

"Hm."

He falls silent for a time and watches as I dip my kabobs in little bowls of *nuoc cham* and nip them off their skewers. He mimics me, eating more delicately. His lips glide across the crisped chicken, which leaves a damp sheen on his skin. I want to lick it off, even more at his low, sinful sound of appreciation.

I'd be happy to let the subject drop and enjoy the meal, but after his kabobs vanish, he points out, "Last night, you apologized for prying."

He breaks apart his disposable wooden chopsticks and gathers a trailing skein of noodles. I say nothing, when I should respond with the proper thing. The human thing: that I'd felt bad for prodding the open wound and stepping into something indelicate.

Yet the truth spills from me before I can stop it. "Only because it's what I'm supposed to say. It's what's expected of me. I've learned to play along to avoid...friction, I suppose."

"So I'm to believe any feelings of remorse, regret, shame,

sorrow—they're all only societal obligations?"

"I can't tell you what to believe, Sean."

I snap my chopsticks apart, breaking them at the base. The loud *crack* echoes over the restaurant, and suddenly I feel like everyone is staring at me. Everyone knows I'm an aberrant, and they're only waiting for me to show my vulnerable underbelly so they can take me down like the animal I am. Paranoia. Comes with the territory. Sometimes I wake from nightmares that Congress has gotten its act together enough to stop fighting with each other and push through aberrant registration, identification, tests that require me to pass a genetic screening just to walk down the street or risk being locked away.

But even if we're standing on the verge of that world, even if I sweat when a security guard or police officer looks at me too long, that won't happen. Not as long as I do my job. I make myself relax, but even I can see the tension in my hands, the way the tendons stand out against my skin as I grip the chopsticks.

"Interesting," Sean murmurs. He won't quite look at me. "You know…I don't think you ever found me frightening. I do think there's something frightening about you, though. There's a change that comes over you, when you realize someone is watching you. You lie so very easily."

"What am I lying about?"

"I don't know." He twirls his noodles around his chopsticks. His pensive gaze follows his fingers. "But you *are* lying. I know it, but I still can't accept that any man can live the way you do."

"You don't have to accept anything. It is what it is."

He still won't look at me, but I can't look away from him. I practically dare him to meet my eyes. Can he see me for what I am? I suddenly want him to. I want him to see me—really see *me*, the monster, the aberrant. I want him to know how beautiful he is…and how much more beautiful he would be if I could leave marks of pain and blood all over his body, see the strain and torment rippling through him. I want to possess him. I want to destroy him.

No.

I want to scare him away.

As much as I don't want this ache building in my throat, I want even less to feel the strange combination of guilt and elation, pain and pleasure, that I know will come when his blood is on my hands and his eyes are glassy and blank. I need him out of my life, out of my thoughts, off my radar. I don't want him to be involved with Langdon. I don't want to face the possibility of killing him.

There's something inside me that doesn't want to, and I don't understand it.

"Are you afraid of me?" I ask.

His gaze snaps to mine, and I catch a flicker of uncertainty. "Not yet," he says. "But I am very, very intrigued."

"I'm your student. Not your rebound."

His next breath hitches. The hurt in his eyes is delicious and terrible. "I know that." Cool. Withdrawn. I've stung him, and whatever walls he'd started to lower for me are coming back up again. "Forgive me for thinking it would be nice to have someone to talk to, for once."

"I'm not much of a conversationalist." Standing, I shrug into my coat. "I need to go back to the lab. Thank you for lunch, Sean."

He starts to stand but sinks back down in his seat. "Are you only saying that because it's expected of you?"

"Yes."

He's so close, yet we look at each other across an immeasurable distance. I want to apologize for hurting him, and I might even mean it. I don't want to find out. I can't do this. I can't have friends, especially friends who make me want to kiss them, touch them, find out if I really can choose to be something else just because they believe I can. He has no idea. He thinks it's all theory, all speculation, but for me it's real. I have no choice, and I don't need someone like him thinking he can save me with his idealism.

As if anything can save me. As if anything could change me.

But if I change, it will be on my own terms. Not for a pair of liquid green eyes.

I have to get out of here. Away from these humans, away from the building frustration and longing and hurt twisting inside me until I'm a tangled mess. I have to get away from *him*.

Before *frustration* becomes something else. Something terrible. Something hungry. Something bloody and dark, lashing out to score my confusion into fragile human flesh.

He looks away first. Wariness clouds his pale eyes. "Finals review on Monday, Tobias. Do try to stay awake."

"Of course," I say, then walk out of the restaurant without looking back.

Langdon is already at the lab when I return. I'm in no mood to listen when he chews me out for being twenty-six minutes late then starts on my jeans and T-shirt with a lecture about professionalism in the workplace. I ignore him, swap my jacket for the lab coat, and retrieve the next batch of test slides.

"No." Langdon stops me with a hand on the tray. "Don't touch them. I'll review them myself."

His beady eyes are suspicious, his mouth twisted into a narrow frown. I force a blank, puzzled look and a careless shrug. "Okay. What am I working on, then?"

"Feed the mice." He sniffs. "I've already taken their

samples. There's no more damage you can do."

I frown. "I don't understand, Dr. Langdon."

"Of course you don't understand. Your clumsiness has ruined my research! Months of testing, and your incompetence has skewed the results!" Langdon gestures wildly, fingers stabbing outward. "I'll have to start over!"

"Sir, I've taken the utmost care and followed proper procedure—"

"*Proper procedure*?" he shrieks. "The tests cannot have simply failed. Not so often. My theory is flawless."

His theory isn't flawless. It's promising, but even without my interference he's only wandering around the ballpark, nowhere close to a home run; I just can't risk he'll accidentally stumble into a swing and knock one out of the park. Telling him his theories and experimentation methods are wrong won't calm him down, though. I bow my head in appropriate shame and contrition.

"I'm sorry, Doctor."

Langdon sneers, and I want to see his rubbery mouth stretched wide in a bloody, deep-cut smile. "If you think I'll approve you as a doctoral candidate, you're dreaming. You're lucky I don't have you expelled." Turning away, he flicks his fingers in that dismissive gesture that makes my blood burn. "Feed the animals. It's all you're good for."

"Of course." I leave the room quickly.

If I don't, I'll give in to the urge to light him up like a Christmas tree.

The animal lab smells of the dry, loamy scent of food pellets, mingled with the clean scent of cedar shavings and the fouler smell of mouse and rat feces. Row upon row of cages are stacked into a bank against the far wall, each labeled with handwritten cards in plastic holders. Yesterday's test group is in the second row: first the unmodified control mouse, then six more injected with variations of the latest viral carrier and corrective genome. The rows below are the failed test groups from the past two weeks, kept for observation. The top row is untouched, waiting for today's tests. There are never more than ten rows of mice in the stack. I never ask what Langdon does with the older mice. Probably disposes of them.

He'll have a lot more to dispose of very shortly.

I have to work quickly. Metal cages. This should make my job easy. I lace my fingers in the wires of one of the center cages and release my power in careful surges, each ripple of electricity crackling in my veins with a sting so sharp it's a sick sort of pleasure, stealing my breath. It can't touch the control mice; I have to restrain myself. Brief static shimmers along the conductive metal bars and electrifies the trays beneath. The mouse in front of me stiffens, its pink eyes widening. Its soft white fur smokes. With a distressed chitter, it twitches, struggling to move, trembling in the grip of rigor.

Then it falls over. Dead.

The current spreads in a radius of pained squeaks and dying bodies. I stop before they're all dead. The untested mice in the top row and the control mice in the end column are still alive. I have to finish a few test mice off one at a time. Quick taps, and they're done. There's only a subtle odor of singed fur, hidden beneath the acidic stink of feces. I dig the feed scoop out of the bag, scatter pellets on the floor, then drop the scoop with a loud clatter.

"Dr. Langdon," I shout. "Dr. Langdon!"

I start for the door just as it opens. With an impatient sneer, he leans in and snaps, "What is it n—"

He stops when he sees the little white corpses, motionless in their cages. He blanches, his mouth going loose.

"I don't know what happened," I babble, and clutch at the front of my lab coat. Agitation. Distress. Near panic. I need him to believe I'm terrified my academic career is over and genuinely upset over a threat to his research. Need him to see me as hapless, rather than a calculating killer timing every play of emotion across my face, in my voice, throughout that body language that shapes so much of how people see me. "Th-they were fine when I left last night. Did... Did you check them before you left?"

He drifts to the cages and presses his hands flat against the bars. "My research," he whispers, his eyes wide, his mouth slack, lines of shock carved into his waxy flesh. "How could this happen?"

"I-I don't know. Was there a contaminant in the carrier cultures? Maybe long-term side effects—" I clap a hand over my mouth. "What if one of the viral carriers jumped and went airborne?"

Anger flashes in his eyes. "You really are a fool. If it's long-term, the animals would die in waves, not at—"

It's so obvious, the moment comprehension clicks and the puzzle pieces fall into place. He turns to face me with wooden movements. A skeletal finger thrusts out, accusing. His eyes are stark, wild.

"You. You did this." He stalks closer, that judging finger nearly jabbing between my eyes. "You've been ruining everything from the start."

I seize his hand and bend it back until he shrieks: high and watery, shrill counterpoint to the satisfying *crack* of popping joints and bone. "I wish you hadn't said that."

It's a lie.

I'm going to enjoy this far, far more than I should.

Chapter Five

The paramedics say it's a stress-induced heart attack. The defibrillator does nothing but make the body jerk, a puppet that only mimics life. Twenty minutes ago he'd jerked the same way—only then, he'd been alive. Alive and struggling to move his mouth enough to let out the screams I could see building behind his eyes, when I shorted out his central nervous system and paralyzed him—until he could only suffer through the slow agony of tiny shocks of electricity worming their way through his body. Bursting his cells from within, the same way I had with the slides. It won't show on the surface.

But it felt good in a way that Sean's simple *morals* would tell me I should be ashamed of.

Part of me had wanted to ask him *why*. To hold him in my grip and force an answer from him that would make his hatred make sense, that would give it a more logical reason than his fear of change, fear of humanity losing their dominant position in the world. Something that would help me *understand*. I've never been able to, and I've often wondered if history would have painted an entirely different picture if the first aberrants had been treated with kindness rather than fear, panic, suspicion.

But I didn't waste my breath. Nothing he could have said would have satisfied me — and had I asked then, killing him would have left me frustrated rather than focused on doing everything necessary to clean up his mess and make sure the crime scene was perfect.

It's all about the subtleties. A brush against the defibrillator's control box in passing, just a few amps of current, are all it takes to break a circuit. A palm pressed to the chest, a brief shock, are all I need to stop a human heart. I could have fried Langdon where he stood, leaving only a crisped husk, but there's no need. Blazes of lightning and arcs of electricity may be impressively theatrical, and reducing Langdon to ash might have been even more satisfying than watching him suffer with that slow, crawling pain...

But if I'd indulged, I wouldn't have been able to call 911 and pass this off as anyone's fault but my own.

He's pronounced dead on the scene. When the paramedics hear my story, they call the CDC and lock down the animal lab, breathing through paper air masks the entire time. They don't give me one. I don't blame them. If there's a viral outbreak, I'm already a vector. But their distraction gives me time to copy Langdon's files to a thumb drive and wipe the primary hard drive with a focused pulse. The latest test slides are ruined in seconds, cells bursting at my touch. Langdon never kept hard-copy files here, too afraid of other faculty members stealing his precious research. His home might be another matter. I'll have to find out, come nightfall.

By the time the paramedics emerge from the animal lab, I'm back in the chair they left me in, huddled inside my jacket and looking appropriately shell-shocked and miserable.

"Tobias?" one of the EMTs says. Her name tag says *J. Andrews*. She's a short, spare woman with a girlishly round face and fresh, innocent eyes. I wonder how much blood she'll have to see before those eyes go dull and tired, like her partner's. Her voice is muffled by her mask. "There's nothing to worry about, but I'd like to take you to the hospital to check you out. The CDC's coming to sweep for biological contaminants and disease vectors, but I need to make sure you haven't been exposed."

"E-exposed?" I stammer. "Exposed to what?"

I can tell she's smiling by the way her mask moves. From her eyes, it's an insipid smile. "Probably nothing. It's not likely that anything could jump from a mouse to a human. But since they're transgenic, we'd like to be safe." She pats my knee. "You'll be fine."

"Are you sure?"

"Absolutely. But I'll need you to breathe through this mask for now. Just in case."

Her partner gives her a look, then me—a look that says he's had the same train of thought as me: that if there's anything wrong, I'm likely already infected. I can see it in his eyes, weighing whether he should crush her idealism and compassion now or take the route that's easier in the short-term but just makes it harder later: indulging her, for now. It'll just make it that much harder to crush her later. I wonder, as he sighs and hands me the mask with a long-suffering look, if he's just doing it to spare himself a little longer.

Or if there's something inside him, too, that will savor the moment when reality breaks her and that bright cheerfulness crumples into something broken that can never be whole again.

I fit the mask over my face while they start noting down their report. They're practically doing my job for me. To the paramedics, I'm just a victim of unfortunate circumstances: an innocent lab tech exposed to the side effects of a scientist's reckless experimentation. They don't even call the police. The

CDC will likely burn everything in the animal lab to destroy any trace of infectious material. If they keep tissue samples for testing, I may have to use my father's connections to retrieve them. That shouldn't be a problem. I've taken care of the most recent data. Once I get Langdon's personal copies, I should have this all wrapped up by tonight.

Perfect.

Keeping my head down, I let the paramedics usher me from the building and into the ambulance. Langdon is a stiff shape inside a black rubber bag, barely glimpsed on the way out, left where he fell on the floor. I stare at it, trying to will myself to feel something. Anything. Trying to choose to be human—but there's nothing there.

Nothing save guilt that I don't feel anything at all.

"Now, this might sting a little," Miss Andrews says, and presses a needle to my inner elbow.

Sting a little. It hurts like hell, but I savor the pain as the needle drives deep into my flesh.

It's the only way to atone, after all.

It's dusk by the time they let me out. I've been poked, prodded, probed in unmentionable places, put through X-rays and CAT scans and EEGs. All they found was one healthy young man with a temperature less than half a degree above normal. It takes a full genetic assay to tell an aberrant from a human, and California's one of the only states that successfully fought back against legislation regarding mandatory genetic screening. The most abnormal thing they find about me is that I actually have health insurance.

My car is still at the lab. I'll have to walk or take the bus. I'm nearly to the corner bus kiosk when a sleek Kawasaki Concours pulls up to the curb, its finish gleaming like hematite. I know those long legs and wide shoulders even before the rider removes his helmet and shakes his hair loose. He straddles that thing like he wants it to submit, and I can't help a faint, prickling chill.

"Sean?" I stare at him. "What are you doing here?"

He shoves the kickstand down and stands, dropping the keys into the pocket of his leather jacket. "I heard about Langdon," he says breathlessly. "I stopped by the lab, and those CDC fellows said you'd been taken here. I was worried."

"Why?"

He looks confused. "Should I not be?"

Now *I'm* confused. Why is he doing this? "Do you come rushing to the hospital for all your students?"

Or are you worried about what I know? Did Langdon say anything to you?

"Can't say I've been in this situation before, but I take your drift." He looks down. His face reflects in the mirror shine of the helmet in his hands. "I suppose it was instinct to be concerned."

"Don't do this." Stepping closer, I catch his wrist. Warm leather, warmer flesh, imprinting on my palm. "I don't know what kind of connection you think we made yesterday, but I told you. I won't be your rebound."

His jaw tightens into a hard line. Glimmers of anger bring a lovely light to his eyes, a becoming flush to his cheeks. "What makes you so certain that's what I want?"

"Because I've seen the way you look at me—and I've seen this a hundred times. You get dumped. Some guy's nice to you when you're vulnerable, and you transfer your affection onto him because you're lonely and want to feel loved."

"Loved? By someone who claims to be so amoral he might as well be heartless? How stupid do you think I am?" He pulls his arm from my grip. "Yes, I am lonely. Yes, I do want to feel loved. That hasn't changed through a dozen failed relationships. But I'm a bloody grown man—older than you. I know better than to throw myself at one of my students, and I don't need you to psychoanalyze me just to remind me of my *place* with you. Why can't you accept genuine concern for what it is?"

"Because I don't understand it. People are inherently self-serving. You. Me. Everyone. No one does anything without some personal motive. There's no such thing as genuine concern."

The prideful tilt of his chin can't hide that I've hurt him. Again. It's there in the creases in the corners of his mouth, in the purse of his lips. "I'm glad I don't live in your world, Tobias. It must be a terrible place."

He turns away. I sigh and rake my hand through my hair. "I'm sorry, Sean."

With a brittle laugh, he stops. "Don't say it if you don't mean it." He tosses the helmet at me. "Come on. I'll give you a ride back to your car."

I fumble to catch the helmet but don't say a word. Sometimes, silence is best.

I don't know what I'd say, anyway. He makes no sense to me. I've upset him. Insulted him. Hurt him.

And yet here he is, waiting for me.

I don't know what to do with that.

I don't know what to do with *him*, or the way everything about him tugs at me like he's trying to pull my slow-beating, quiet heart through my chest.

Riding with his hips clasped between my thighs, the motorcycle snarling beneath us, is the hardest thing I've ever done.

The inside of the helmet smells like him: clove cigarettes and something caramel-sweet and a certain earthy, masculine musk, just a hint of aftershave. His body is warm, even through the jacket. The smoothness of him always made me think he'd be soft, yielding, but under the jacket he's firm and toned, his stomach taut beneath my clasped hands. My fingers burn to wander, but I clench them together. The temptation is almost too much.

I may be an aberrant, but I'm still a man.

I haven't been with anyone in a long time. Mostly Jeremy. Kalen. A few casual flings. Jeremy was easiest. Dad trusts him because he's discreet. I went to him for the same reasons. He doesn't ask questions, and doesn't care how much I hurt him. He just took what he wanted, gave me what I wanted, and that was the end of it. With other aberrants, there's little risk of emotional attachment. He always left in the morning. I never asked him to stay.

Sean would want to stay. Sean would beg me not to be so rough. Sean would be upset, would ask me why, would look at me with those keen eyes and begin to suspect. It's best that I put these thoughts out of my head.

Thank the *narakas* it's a short ride back to the lab. The CDC vans are still lined up in front of the science building. The lights are still on in the upstairs windows. They'll probably be in there all night, sweeping the place. All it takes is one incident and the CDC thinks it's *Outbreak* and starts looking for the contaminated monkey.

Sean kills the engine. I shouldn't linger, but I do. My hips fit against him just right. My jeans are a little too tight, and heat builds with a low drawing ache between my thighs. I take a deep breath, memorizing the scent inside the helmet, then take it off and pass it forward. He accepts it without a word. The motorcycle's quivering growl has left my legs stiff and half-numb, but I pry myself off and stand.

I expect him to drive off—but he stays, looking down at the helmet in his hands. He wants to say something. I can see it in the set of his mouth, in the way his downcast eyes look at anything but me. He won't speak until I do. Humans are like that, with their social cues that play like a game of call and response, giving away their feelings in the hopes of getting something in return. UC Berkeley is the first time I've lived among humans since my mother died, but over the years I've learned to read the emotions they think they hide so well...even if I can't understand them. I've embarrassed him, wounded him, spat on the hand he offered me, and the worst part? I don't care.

Don't say it if you don't mean it.

If he's as proud as I think he is, he won't say a word.

I tell myself to walk away. I've achieved my purpose. Sean thinks I'm an asshole. Whether his interest in me is friendly or something more, he won't try to get any closer. He'll stop trying to make me be something I'm not. Strictly student and teacher. All I have room for. All I have time for, when tonight I have work to do. One murder to plan. Another to clean up.

I am my father's son, and I can only do my father's work.

"Sean."

He lifts his head, looking at me with guarded question, his eyes as cold as jade ice.

I manage a smile. "Are you doing anything tonight?"

Chapter Six

"I shouldn't be here with you."

His voice goes almost unheard beneath the quiet sounds of the night. We sit side by side on the tumbled rocks sloping down from Eastshore Freeway to the bay. From here we can see the San Francisco lights, brighter than the stars, glimmering on water as slick as oiled silk. The breeze and lapping waves are louder than the cars that make a river of taillights on the Bay Bridge. I watch Sean from the corner of my eye. He leans back on his hands and tilts his face to the sky. The moon licks his throat with a greedy silver tongue and turns his glasses into mirrors.

"You could have said no," I point out.

"I should have." In the shadows, his eyes are no less luminous. They're unnatural, and continue to draw me back time and time again. "As you're so fond of pointing out, you're my student. Not only that, but you're cruel, arrogant, and presumptuous."

The first two, I'll own. But— "Presumptuous?"

"To think I was flirting with you. I do have professional

ethics, you know." With a half smile, he fiddles with the cuff of his jacket. "Not that you would understand that."

It takes a moment to realize he's teasing. I chuckle. "I suppose I wouldn't. Any more than I can understand these things you call concern and compassion."

His smile fades. "You're a very strange man, Tobias. No concept of compassion, yet you take pity on a lonely schoolteacher and offer companionship."

"It's not pity."

"Then what is it?"

I shrug. "I'm curious. I don't have any friends, so it's a little difficult for me to recognize when someone's trying to be one."

"With your charming personality, I find that hard to believe," he mutters with a dry laugh, then sighs. "I really don't get you, you know. This shy, quiet man who sleeps through my class turns out to be a cold cynic. You mock me at one turn, invite me the next…but if I reach out to you, you run away. You're a complete contradiction."

"Should I point out again that you like contradictions?"

"Mm. You've got me there. That doesn't mean I can't wonder why you contradict yourself."

"Whim." Even now it's an act, nonchalant and flippant. "Though that's not why I don't pay attention in class."

"I suppose I'll regret asking why."

"It's hard to listen to what you're *saying* when I'm distracted just listening to *you*."

He falters. His lower lip creeps between his teeth, and his brows knit. "If you think that's funny, you're sadly mistaken."

"Honest answer to an honest question. If you don't want to know, don't ask."

His mouth twists up, before he lets out an explosive sigh. "You are entirely, infuriatingly baffling."

"And that," I say, "is exactly the point."

He laughs, low and tired, almost a concession, a surrender. "Now I see. International man of mystery, are you? As long as you keep me off-balance, I'll never discover your terrible secrets."

"You're catching on." And I'll never let him know how close he is to the truth. I need a diversion. A different subject, one that doesn't hit so close to home. I draw my jacket around me and zip it up. "It's damned freezing out here."

"Ninny. You'd never survive an English winter." He shrugs out of his coat, as if to prove a point. His bare arms pull taut as he leans back on them, biceps cut stark and something about the sharp angle of his radial muscles making my knees feel strange. "You California boys just can't stand the cold."

"I'm not from California."

"Oh? Then where?"

"Georgia. Or..." *Don't say it.* My heart does an odd little flip. "Or Thailand. Take your pick. I'm surprised you couldn't tell by the accent."

Not that I have much of one anymore. My mother taught me Thai, but my father spoke American English, always. Guess which one I had more time to absorb.

"Thailand? Oh." Sean's voice softens. He leans just a touch closer, his warmth prickling at me. "I see. Did you leave after the disaster?"

It's so easy to lie and tell the truth at the same time. Careful omissions that make the story seem like something other than what it is; that make it sound like it belongs to someone else so I don't have to feel anything when I say, "Yes. I lived there with my mother."

"Until...she died?"

"Yeah." I wonder what Sean would think, if he knew how she died. If he knew just who her murderer was. "My father's American. You've probably heard of him. He owns practically every Burger Café in the country. After Thailand burned, I came to the States. He raised me."

It's someone else's story. Someone else's truth when Berkeley is the first life I've known outside of Xinth, and no one raised me but my father's attendants—but the pain is mine, moving clumsily in my chest, ill-used and yet still managing to stab its spikes everywhere.

I don't expect to feel a hand on my arm. I don't expect to *need* a hand on my arm, but that touch drifting over my jacket reminds me that he's there. Anchors me. Holds me down and refuses to let me wiggle away from the crack opening inside me, though I don't want to look and see what's trying to get out. Whatever it is, it hurts with a dull, throbbing pain that makes my heart feel too heavy.

I don't want it.

"I'm so sorry, Tobias," he says. "It's terrible, what happened over there."

I shrug, keeping my gaze fixed on the water. "It's fine. I barely remember her. Just her name. Hathai. 'Heart.' Like… like she was our heart, but…it's been me and Dad for a long time now, and I'm not sure we have much heart left."

Another lie. I do remember her. She smelled like rain. I see her when I look in the mirror. Same face. Same black hair, same black eyes, same pale, gold-touched skin. I am aberrant, but she was human—and it's a human who stares back at me through her eyes, asking me just what I've let myself become.

The water's reflective surface throws my thoughts back at me with a dark gloss. Its damp, rhythmic splashes laugh at me. I want to break it, but it would be futile. Force has no effect on water. Push it away, and it only flows to fill a new place. Fate is like water: inexorable, unstoppable, sometimes calm, sometimes turbulent, always inescapable. Push your fate away, and it flows to fill the spaces around you until you're surrounded.

Drowning.

Sean is still looking at me, quiet expectation without demand. I sigh and force myself to speak, to answer that human need for something to fill the silence. "Sometimes it feels like it'll always be just us," I murmur. "He's already planned my whole future for me. I suppose one day I'll take his place, and turn into him. With Langdon dead, I doubt I'll get another position in the lab. No doctorate. Which means home to Dad. Back to the place he's made for me."

"You don't sound very happy about that."

I smile. It hurts my face, like it was carved into my flesh. "Who wouldn't be happy about having an empire handed to them?"

"Someone who wants to be his own man." His hand is still on my arm, as if it belongs there. "You're an adult. Your life is your own, not his. Shape it how you please."

"And if I don't have that choice?"

"Tobias." He draws on my arm, urging me to face him. "We all have that choice."

"I don't," I say, and kiss him.

I tell myself I do it to silence him. This is too personal, too invasive. His questions stray too close to the weakness at the heart of me, and I can't stand any more. Yet in truth, I do it because I want to; I've wanted to since the first taste of his laughter, since I felt his body clasped between my thighs. Sean tenses with a startled sound. I expect him to pull away, yet his mouth is firm and full against mine, his lips parting in an invitation he may regret. Weaving my fingers into his hair, I drag him close, fisting a handful of cool black strands. I feel his shiver like a delicious thrill as I taste him, chasing the heady flavor of cloves and the luscious, damp heat that is purely Sean.

His arms wrap around me with surprising strength, fingers smoothing against my back. His teeth are fierce against my lower lip, nipping until I taste the metallic flavor of a bruise blending between our mouths. Before I can catch my breath, his lips dominate mine, seizing control and plundering my mouth with such intimate heat that my gut tightens, and I cannot stop the moan that wells in my throat. I'd never thought him capable of such aggression. No one else has ever dared. One must always submit to the Lord High General's son.

Yet here, I am only Tobias. Here I let Sean kiss me until fire melts through me, and my will turns soft and pliant in a way I've never allowed before. Only when I can no longer breathe do I break back, licking my kiss-swollen, pulsing lips. He looks down at me with a small, unreadable smile, his eyes dark.

"I thought you said you weren't flirting with me," I murmur.

He chuckles, something husky and hungry edging the sound. "That doesn't mean I didn't want to." His smile twists into a frown. "But I should not have done that."

"I started it."

"Yes. And it puzzles me that you did." Leaning back, he lets his arms fall and shakes his head. "I meant what I said. I'm not looking for a rebound, or even a fling. That was never my intent—"

I stop him with a finger to his lips. "I know. Don't overanalyze it. I'm attracted to you. You're attracted to me. Let it be simply that."

Sighing, he lifts his gaze to the bridge. "The question is… what are we to do about it?"

That, I don't know. Nothing; that's what I should say. Yet as the wind fingers his hair, teasing it across his face in ever-shifting patterns of black and white, I want to kiss him again. I want to feel his savagery again, taste the aggression on his lips.

And again, that means I need to leave.

Unfolding to my feet, I straighten my coat. "Maybe I'll

tell you later."

He looks like he's just been slapped. "Where are you going?"

"I have an appointment." I climb up the rocky slope toward the road. We took his motorcycle to the waterfront, but my apartment is close by. No point in going back for my car, which is still parked at the lab.

"On foot? At this time of night?" he calls after me. "Are you daft?"

"It's good exercise." Stopping at the edge of the road, I flick off a quick salute. "See you in class, Sean."

"Sure." His voice is barely audible. "See you."

I leave him like that, forlorn and alone. I know what he must be thinking: I've just toyed with him and walked off, gratifying a whim without a care for how he feels. It would be better if he were right. Rebound or not, he was just dumped last night. That's an emotional minefield I don't know how to navigate. Relationships are not my forte.

Not to mention getting entangled with a human again, especially my professor, is a very bad idea. I've already killed one faculty member. One is an accident.

Two would be a murder investigation, and a trail of bodies leading straight to me.

My apartment isn't far. Just under two miles. By the time I reach home, I'm too cold to think about Sean or anything but a hot shower to wash away the feeling of so many human hands poking and prodding me with their latex-gloved fingers. Samadhi's yowling drags me out of the hot spray. I dry off and wrap a towel around my waist. Usually I come home in the afternoons to feed her. I'm lucky she didn't take a crap on the couch to punish me for making her wait.

"All right, all right, you walking gullet." I dump a fresh can of wet food into her bowl and get a nose full of bushy tail for my troubles. "Wretch."

It's just after eight. A little too early for me to be playing cat burglar on a Saturday night. The Berkeley nightlife is just winding up, and someone might spot me engaging in a few acts of breaking and entering. I get dressed anyway, retrieving a garment bag from the back of the closet and unzipping it on the bed to spill my gear out across the duvet.

The idea of a villain's costume probably seems ludicrous, but when I change I truly feel like a different person. I wouldn't call Spark my alter ego, but when I wear his face, I'm more free to be what an aberrant should be. Cold. Ruthless. Unstoppable. The mask doesn't just hide my identity as Tobias Rutherford. It makes my identity as Spark visible to the world, along with everything Spark represents as the iron fist of the aberrant rebellion. A blade wielded by my father's heavy hand, a weapon with no will other than that of its owner.

Dad leans toward flamboyant military styles, complemented by a cape with a black flame motif. My tastes are simpler; I had to vote against Miss Vida Boheme and choose substance over style. Well-worn black jeans, the denim stretched as soft as silk, give me comfort and flexibility. Thick-soled combat boots provide traction and shock absorption. A black A-shirt is thin enough to keep me cool in the adrenaline-fueled sweat of combat, counteracting the long black coat. The coat is less a dramatic statement and more a method of protection. In a high-speed fight the coat obscures my shape and makes it harder to target the more vulnerable areas of my body. It shrouds me, makes me harder to recognize, and under cover of darkness it makes me just another shadow, blending into the night unseen.

Like I said, I prefer subtlety to show. The one concession? The silver-blue thread zigzagging from my shoulder to the cuff of my left sleeve, an embroidered bolt of lightning spearing down to splash tailored, stitched sparks over my wrist. Dad had insisted. I'd rolled my eyes. He'd taken that as permission.

He usually does.

Black leather gloves insulate against unwanted electrical accidents. Layered belts and thigh straps keep my tools and weapons close to hand. It's stupid to go out unprepared, relying only on superhuman powers. It takes more than that to survive. It takes more than an empty heart to be what humans would call a villain, a vigilante, a monster, a terrorist. You have to train, both physically and mentally. You must be able to control more than your powers; you must be able to control *yourself*. You must never stop thinking, calculating, planning. There's no freedom to be something as simple as a man.

You must be a killer, body and soul.

A fitted black half mask covers all of my face save my lips and jaw. Very few would remember the elusive, reclusive Tobias Rutherford well enough to match the lower half of his face to the man who looks back at me in the mirror. Spark. There's nothing of my mother in him, not even the eyes. They're too hard, too dead, wiped blank by the things they've seen.

I'm glad my mother died before she could see me like this.

Would Sean recognize me? Would he see my lips bruised so red and full from his kiss and know me for what I am? Perhaps he'd understand, then. You can't teach an aberrant about morals, or ethics. We have the capacity for neither. But I wonder, as I slip out the window...

Am I trying to convince him, or myself?

I scale the fire escape to the roof, boots moving soundlessly on the grating. The wind cuts me, but I don't mind. It's a different feeling when I become Spark. Exhilarating. Every sensation is keen, almost too stark. I breathe in the night's scents—food and diesel exhaust and human sweat and filth—and breathe out purity. Power flows through me like smoke, reminding me that I am an animal and the world is my prey. It's better than any cigarette, even one tasted on Sean's lips.

Damn it. My mind is wandering again. I yank myself back on track and set out across the rooftops. Above the city it's like my own personal highway, moving above the crass glare of the lights and the slow-moving herd of human traffic. I leap from one roof to the next, swing down to fire escapes, scale rain gutters. No one sees me. No one ever thinks to look up.

Oblivious. People are oblivious to the world that moves in tandem to their own, convinced that if they don't see it, it doesn't exist.

I know where Langdon's house is from the many times he made me haul lab equipment. It's in one of the smaller Berkeley suburbs, a poor man's gated community where squat little adobe houses try to look resplendent on their carefully parceled squares of grass. There's little cover here. I stick to the backyards, out of sight of the main street and sweeping headlights. Tool sheds, playpens, and shoddy fences hide me. Before long I crouch against the wall of Langdon's house, concealed in its shadow.

A van is parked in the drive, CENTERS FOR DISEASE CONTROL emblazoned on its side. Shit. They're earlier than I'd expected. I'd planned to bide my time, scope out the security system, wait until the neighborhood bedded down for the night. I might not have that option now—especially when I spot the motorcycle parked on the street, behind the van.

Sean.

Chapter Seven

The lights are on inside. Shadows move against the living room window. I creep forward and risk a quick peek through the window. Sean leans against the frame of the open front door, looking uneasy; a surgical mask conceals the lower half of his face. I count two men in hazmat suits, faceplates down but their oxygen masks firmly in place. I can hear the faint sounds of them canvassing the house, but nothing else. I edge around to the front of the building and flatten myself against the wall near the door. Voices drift through.

"I still don't feel right letting you in here," Sean says. What the hell is he *doing* here? "He hasn't been dead twenty-four hours, and you're looting."

"We aren't looting, sir," one of the CDC men says. "We're searching for evidence of a potential biomedical threat or biological terrorism." He sounds so bored it's obvious even he doesn't think Langdon could have been a terrorist, brewing up bioweapons for the aberrants or ISIS or Boko Haram or this week's latest flavor of human terribleness. "We apologize for disrupting your evening. We'll finish as quickly as possible."

"I'm not even supposed to have this key. The dean will hang me. What if there's a police investigation?"

"We'll take full responsibility for any liability. Thank you for your cooperation."

Langdon's spare house key. I'd forgotten it. He'd kept it taped in the third drawer of his desk. I wasn't even supposed to know about it, but I'd stumbled across it while searching for a spare refracting lens. I can't believe I overlooked it. Stupid.

But how did Sean know about it?

Footsteps warn me in time to duck around the side of the house and conceal myself again. The two men emerge, one carrying a laptop and a tray of slides, the other a bulky desktop tower. They load it all into the back of the van, then disappear into the house again. This is my only chance.

I make a break for it, across the lawn. For a moment I'm exposed in the bright moonlight on the treeless grass. For those seconds I hold my breath, heart pounding. Then I slither into the back of the van and close the doors soundlessly behind me. The van's interior is a jumble of equipment, barely outlined by light filtering through the front windows.

Crouching next to the desktop tower, I pull my glove off with my teeth and lay my hand against the cold metal. A quick surge should be enough to fry the insides beyond hope of recovery. I don't have time for finesse. I do the same with the laptop, power tingling through my fingertips, and let the excess static discharge take care of the slides.

Muffled voices tell me they're coming back. I throw myself into the backseat of the van and hide in the dark crawlspace below the seat. The rear doors open.

"That the last of it, Pete?"

"Looks like. You check upstairs?" There's a dull *thud* that bounces the van on its tires.

"Yeah. Nothing but porn. Let's wrap it up and head out."

Sean's voice is more distant, muted, but drawing closer.

"Should I just lock up here?"

"That should work fine, sir." A pause. "If you or your colleagues find anything significant regarding Dr. Langdon's research, specifically anything related to infectious substances, please call this number."

"Certainly."

The doors slam closed again. I keep myself completely still while the CDC men let themselves into the driver's and passenger seats. The engine starts. The van rocks and jounces down the street. I'm stuck here, for now. If I move, they'll see me. They're so close I can hear their breathing. The one in the passenger seat—I think it's Pete—lowers his mask and belches. Even from down here, it smells like hot dogs and unwashed feet.

"I hate these late shifts."

"Yeah, but you know how the director gets. He's got a bug up his ass about these viral carriers and disease potential. Just an hour in the lab, and we can wrap it up and go home."

"Like hell. There's a strip club with my name on it."

The driver sighs. "It's your paycheck."

With breath like that, I pity the strippers.

I may have to kill these two. It's risky. If two people directly connected to the investigation of a dead scientist's research disappear the night of his death, it will be too suspicious, too conspicuous—and the idea of adding two more to the growing body count leaves an odd, heavy feeling in the pit of my stomach.

If I'm exposed, I'll likely have to abandon my cover and go back to my father, but it's a risk I'll have to take. I can't let them learn anything significant about Langdon's research. Even if I destroy the evidence later, all it takes is the wrong words in the wrong ears to start a widespread effort to recreate an aberrant cure.

Luck turns in my favor when they stop for gas half an

hour later. The driver gets out and starts the pump. Pete heads into the store. I climb into the rear storage area. There's a cardboard box of files labeled in Langdon's scratchy hand, a spool of DVD-RWs, an external hard drive, and several thumb drives. I shove the DVDs and thumb drives into the inner pockets of my coat, and fry the hard drive with a single jolt.

Soft metallic clanks. The driver is fiddling with the gas tank. Pete isn't back yet. I wait until I hear the driver screw the gas cap on and move away. Hefting the box of files under my arm, I ease the back door open and peer out. Clear avenue of escape. It's just a short way to the alley next to the gas station. I slither out into the bright halogen lights and bolt for it. No shouts follow me. No pounding feet. I'm clear, and I spend a few moments pressed to the graffiti-sprayed brick just past the alley's mouth, panting for mouthfuls of gasoline-scented breath, before I slip off into the night.

In an abandoned lot behind a condemned building, I burn the files and the box they came in, stirring them until every scrap of paper is nothing but an unreadable flake of ash. The DVDs I snap into pieces and drop through a sewer grate. I keep the thumb drives. Dad's research staff might find them useful.

The street signs tell me I'm on the far side of Oakland, several miles from Langdon's house and my apartment. Farther than I want to walk—and through areas where walking on foot dressed like this will end in a fight whether I want it to or not. I'd walk away from a scuffle, but it would draw unwanted attention. Discretion, better part of valor, the usual.

That's how I end up stripping out of my coat, mask, and gear, and parking my ass on the first bus back to Berkeley. The world-conquering monster on public transit, shivering with my arms out and prickling in the cold night air. With the coat draped to hide the patterned sleeve and my mask and belts concealed in its folds, I'm just another wannabe tough guy walking the streets in his undershirt. That's another reason I prefer this outfit: easy anonymity in a flash.

It's after eleven by the time the bus lets me off a few blocks from Langdon's neighborhood. The CDC already scoured the house, but I won't feel secure until I've checked for myself. I stroll casually for a block or two, hands in my pockets, coat dangling from my arm, and let myself blend into pedestrian traffic. Near Langdon's street, I wander down a side avenue, conceal myself behind a Dumpster, and dress myself. Only when I'm safely hidden behind the veil of Spark again do I slip out and retrace my route to Langdon's front door.

Sean and the CDC have done me a favor. The door is locked, but the security system is disarmed. A slip of wire and a practiced twist pick the lock and let me inside; I catch a whiff of the same faint medicinal smell as the lab, as if it followed Langdon home like a lost puppy. The house is a shambles: books pulled from shelves, drawers hanging open, couch cushions overturned. A tray of DVDs has been spilled over the floor. Most are hentai, with covers detailing naked, underage cartoon girls bound in impossible positions. More tentacles. A *lot* more tentacles. The DVDs are probably as sticky as Langdon's keyboard. I steer clear.

Working in the dark, I search each room, checking places the CDC didn't look—from the upper surfaces of ceiling fan blades to inside the air vents, the back of the stove, the toilet tank. Nothing. The office desk is covered in papers, nothing but grant applications and administrative paperwork. A perfect square of lighter finish on the floor shows where his desktop tower used to be. The CDC left the monitor.

I try the bedroom. Nothing under the mattress, or under the bed. On a desk pushed against the wall, surrounded by stacks of dog-eared hentai manga framing where his laptop should fit, is a Post-it scribbled with a single string of letters.

G8TUI002*6V@mmB

Looks like a password, and it's oddly familiar. Could be useful. The Post-it is taped on all four sides. I peel it off and tuck it into my pocket.

The front door slams. I freeze. The light flicks on with a *click*, casting a square of sallow yellow that just reaches up the stairs to the bedroom. I turn so quickly my elbow hits the stack of manga, and several tumble to the floor.

"Hello?" a voice calls from downstairs. Sean. It's Sean. What is he doing here *again*? "Is anyone there?"

The stairwell light snaps on. Footsteps on creaking stairs. Shit. I bolt for the window, yank it open, and throw myself through. Two stories down, I hit the grass hard and tumble, breath knocked from me with a hard, thumping jolt, leaving my sternum feeling like a snapped Thanksgiving wishbone. Gasping, I roll to my feet and run, losing myself in the darkness between the pooling light of streetlamps only to take to the rooftops again, following my invisible pathways home. I don't think he saw me. As long as he didn't hear me open the window, maybe he'll think the CDC did it. They'd been pretty careless. So had I, but I hadn't expected company.

What could Sean possibly have come back for?

I don't have time to wonder. Halfway back to my apartment, my in-ear headset gives a discreet beep. My phone vibrates in my back pocket. I pause on the roof of a vegan grocery co-op and take the call.

My father's voice is steely. "You booked a holiday vacation? I thought I'd made my expectations clear, son."

"You did. Was I not clear enough myself?"

Silence. He's not used to me talking back, not since I was an angry teenager who wanted nothing more than to have his mother back. He'd channeled my anger, back then. Used it to forge me into what I am now. Calm defiance is new. I blame Sean.

After a moment, Dad says, "You have a right to your objections, but I have reasons for my orders. You could jeopardize a very delicate operation." A cold edge creeps in. "And it was underhanded to let me find out through Jeremy."

"Jeremy's your whipping boy. Not me." I watch a couple stroll by below, hand in hand. The young man pulls free of the girl, only to slide his arm around her waist. Her face is radiant. What must that feel like? "I can't disappear for good. Langdon's dead."

"I didn't authorize that."

"It became necessary. He was growing suspicious. I made it look like a heart attack. No police. It's wrapped up—but if his research assistant skips town for good, it could draw the wrong sort of attention."

"That was careless, son."

"I took care of it. I have his thumb drives. The physical records have been burned, and all his hard drives wiped."

"Networked backups?"

"On my way home to check."

"Very well." He sighs. "We'll talk about it in a few weeks. I'll be in New Hampshire before Christmas."

"What? Why?"

"I told you, this is a delicate operation. It's time I made an appearance in the United States and made a statement. New Hampshire is a good place to start."

Made a statement. For him, that means widespread destruction. A demonstration of power. A demand for submission. I'd known he was planning a big step in advancing his empire, but I didn't think he'd take on a megalithic superpower like America just yet.

"Well," I bite off. "Won't that be grand. A family Christmas."

"I'm in no mood for your flippancy, Tobias." It's jarring, to hear my real name when I wear this mask. "I'd thought I could rely on you—but you seem to be straying, so far from the fold."

"Having my own life is straying? I'm twenty-five, not twelve. You can't make all my decisions for me. Most people my age have a job, a life, a future planned out."

"You're doing your job, son. You have a future. I'm doing everything I can to make it a reality."

"Yeah. I know." And it's the last thing I'd ever want. "Blaze—"

"What is it?"

I should ask him about the incident at the airport. I should tell him to stop meddling in my life. I should tell him a lot of things.

I don't.

"It's nothing." I reach for the headset. "I'll see you in New Hampshire."

When the call ends, I sink down to the roof, letting my legs swing over the edge. It's funny; people never think to look up, but until this moment I've never thought to look down. The city below is a basin catching fallen stars, wreathing Berkeley in halos of light and laughter. These people know what's out there. They know any day their city could fall as Nonthaburi did, as Hat Yai did, Ha Noi and Phnom Penh and Kuching— without warning, without mercy. This city should be dark with fear, its people hidden away, waiting for the day Xinth turns its sights on them. Instead, they laugh and dance beneath the lights as if it's their last night on earth.

It's senseless. It's beautiful. I wonder why I've never noticed before. If my father has his way, this will all become ash. I shouldn't care.

I shouldn't care, but I do.

And I don't know what to do about it.

Chapter Eight

I don't go home for a while. There's nothing waiting for me but a gluttonous cat, an empty bed, and more of Dad's dirty work. I'm tempted to hunt Sean down. I need to know why he came back to Langdon's. He seems much too familiar with Langdon and his routines. He knew where Langdon kept his spare key. He just happened to be the one who let the CDC into Langdon's house. Was he looking for something? Had he left something behind? Were they sleeping together?

Ew.

Maybe I'm being paranoid again. He'd been bothered by the CDC tearing the place apart. Looting, he'd called it. He'd probably come back to clean up. I don't need to see him. It's a bad idea. The worst idea I've ever had.

It's nearly dawn by the time I slip through my bedroom window. Samadhi sprawls on my bed like she knows I need company. More likely she knows I hate brushing her fur off my duvet, but I'm content to shed my costume and curl up in bed with the cat nestled against my hip and my laptop propped on my thigh. I smooth the curled Post-it between my fingers. The tape sticks to my skin, the edges itching.

G8TUI002*6V@mmB. It's too long to be his university computer password. I've watched him type it over and over again, and it's not that long. Maybe for his laptop, or his home PC—but that doesn't seem right. Out of all three computers, why would he only write down the password for this one?

I try the thumb drives. Not one is password-protected, and not a single file contains any information I haven't seen before. Most of them I've prepared myself, mostly analytical comparisons of transgenic mouse slides. The familiarity nags at me. Damn it, I don't have time for this. I should be working out my plan to deal with Senator Cranston, not chasing down Langdon's ghost. I stare at the stained slip of yellow paper.

Stained yellow paper.

Memory flashes. Another Post-it taped to the monitor in the lab, and another on the desk in Langdon's home office. The same string of characters. So familiar I'd looked right over it, at first. He wouldn't use the same password for every computer. It's not his Windows log-in.

It's his email password.

It has to be. With a few taps, I load the university faculty intranet site. I know his email address by heart. I see it often enough, demanding things at all hours of the day and night. I type it in for the user name, then copy in the password and hit enter.

His inbox opens before me: hundreds of messages dating back at least three years, maybe more. He was a data pack rat. Great. So much for my grand plan of scouring his email to see if he'd sent copies of his data anywhere. It's probably pointless. Langdon was more paranoid than I am, terrified of anyone stealing his data and getting a grant—or worse, a patent—before him. He wouldn't share anything vital over email.

I push the idea out of my head and, while I'm logged on

to the faculty intranet, check his network folders. Nothing. Nothing when I try the password and both his personal and work email addresses on Dropbox and OneDrive, either. That paranoia of his meant no files where anyone might get their greedy little hands on his research. I start closing browser tabs. That was a wasted ten minutes, and I need to be more careful. I doubt anyone will start doing the kind of digital forensics that would unearth log-ons from his accounts hours after his official time of death, but even that one-in-a-million chance is a risk I shouldn't take. I start to close the email tab, until a name in the sender column catches my attention.

Cranston, Richard D.

Dozens of emails, all from the last few months. I open the most recent, dated just two days ago.

SUBJECT: Re: Are you ready?

Dr. Langdon:

Please don't waste my time. If I'm to push this through before the end of the year, I need irrefutable evidence, not conjecture. Real data. Real facts. I'm beginning to think you don't want a sponsorship.

Don't disappoint me.

-Rick

My stomach sinks. I check the sent messages. The newest was last night.

SUBJECT: Re: Re: Are you ready?

Threatening me won't make the wheels of science turn faster. I think you'll find the results of my study most satisfying—and illuminating. The data presents inescapable conclusions, and my associate has promised more information very shortly. I look forward to your speech, Senator.

-Dr. Eli Langdon, PhD

Dozens of file names litter the bottom of the email. Attachments. I open documents strewn with statistical charts and comparisons. It takes me a minute to understand what I'm seeing. When I do, I want to throw up, nausea boiling and rolling over my stomach with a sick heat. Langdon has been working on this for years, gathering information from worldwide population metrics and drawing correlations between *in vitro* detection of genetic behavior disorders in infants and the appearance of the aberrant genetic strain. Nearly a 90 percent occurrence, with almost 100 percent of known genetic aberrants turning into a criminal statistic. Medical treatments show zero effect. Medication treats the behavioral disorders, but not the underlying genetic trip wire that causes them and gives rise to these powers.

There's information on Xinth, too, including estimated populations and distribution ratios of behavioral disorders classified as aberrant, triggered by one little twist in the DNA that doesn't just unlock these abilities, but interferes with our hardwired mental chemicals. No gift without a price. I've often wondered if the source of the aberrant strain was man-made. Evolution wouldn't make these kinds of mistakes; wouldn't push us in a potentially nonviable direction in which aberrant genes wreak such havoc in biological function without a care for the side effects. Humans don't understand genetic triggers or gene expression well enough to fuck with them, but they do it anyway.

As one of the documents proves. The file, when I open it, contains a detailed plan for prenatal treatment: a cure that either corrects the aberrant fetus's genetics, or terminates the pregnancy.

Kills the child, rather than bring an aberrant fetus to term.

This isn't about containment. It's not even about control. This is eugenics of the worst kind.

I can't breathe. My chest hurts. I can't believe I'd missed this; there'd been no sign of it in the lab. Langdon must have been working on this on the sly, on his own time, partnering with Senator Cranston to turn his research on an aberrant cure into something more lethal. How lethal depends on what they plan to do with it. I scan through a few more emails. One mentions presenting before Congress during the last week of December.

The last week of December. It won't matter if Cranston dies on New Year's if he signs this into law before he's gone.

Something like this could easily push Cranston's anti-aberrant legislation forward, maybe even garner enough support for a presidential run. With a president indebted to him, Langdon would have had access to all the grants he wanted—enough to fund his cure and completely wipe out the aberrant strain.

We have to step this up. Dad can't have known about this. He'd have had me kill Langdon long ago. Hell, I wish I'd killed him earlier. I knew humans hated us. I never guessed just how far people like Langdon would go. Anything to get rid of aberrants.

Anything to get rid of me.

I can't let Cranston speak before Congress. Not when he has Langdon's surviving research—though I'm not sure killing him is the right choice. Make a martyr out of him, and everything he worked for becomes not politics, but a crusade that his surviving allies will fight for with everything in them. But I can't just ignore him, either. With this data, it'll be a unanimous vote to lock us up, and we'll be lucky if they just throw away the key rather than culling us entirely.

Once the United States starts the witch hunt, other

nations will follow. There'll be no choice for aberrants but Xinth or death, and I have a feeling most of our kind would rather join the fight than wait for it to roll over them and leave them ashes in its wake. Dad won't let us be wiped out. It'll be global war, and he won't be satisfied until everything and everyone burns.

To hell with New Hampshire. I have to go to D.C. I have to stop Cranston before one speech, one law, changes everything.

But first, I have to know how Sean is involved in this.

Chapter Nine

Monday evening. It's warm in the lecture hall, for once. Sean usually keeps it razor cold. To keep us awake, he says. Frankly I think he just enjoys making us physically as well as intellectually uncomfortable. There's a little sadism underneath that calm exterior. There has to be, to be a university professor.

He's Dr. Archer again tonight: neat black slacks, white dress shirt with the sleeves rolled to the elbows, polished shoes. His hair is tied back at his nape, only a few strands falling into his cold, unsmiling face. I'm the only one who knows he's terrified behind those aloofly arched brows, his heart racing, and he can barely breathe. Only I know it's all an act.

I suppose humans wear masks, too.

Tonight I don't doze through class. Tonight I listen to every word and watch him without fail. On the outside he seems composed, smooth. He doesn't even look at me. No—he *won't* look at me. He makes eye contact with every student in class over the course of the lecture, but his gaze skitters over me as if I'm not there. Now and then I catch him fidgeting with a retractable pen, clicking the tip in and out. He's trying to make a point about the thin percentage of genetic difference in mammalian species, but I can tell his heart's not in it.

I can't help a half smile. The moment my mouth quirks, he glances my way. Just a flash, hard and hot and resentful over the reflective shield of his glasses, then away. He's angry with me. That only makes me smile more. Good. If he's angry, he'll be careless. Say the wrong thing.

Tell me exactly what I need to hear.

When class lets out, I remain in my seat and wait for the lecture hall to clear. Sean piles folders and papers into a stack with brisk, jerky motions, his eyes on his work and not on me. I wait. This time, I'll make him speak first.

He slides his things into a leather satchel. His voice could cut diamonds. "Is there something I can help you with, Mr. Rutherford?"

"Class is over. It's Tobias."

His shoulders stiffen. He shoves a sheaf of papers into the bag, crumpling several pages. Good thing I haven't turned in my thesis yet, or he'd probably have run it through a shredder by now. Tucking the slim binder under my arm, I stand and make my way down the tiered seats to his desk. When I offer the binder, he finally meets my eyes, his own puzzled.

"What is this?"

"My semester thesis. Thought I'd turn it in early."

With a frown he takes the folder and, flipping the cover open, reads the title page. "*Aberrant Genetics and the Ethics of Genocide.*" He bites his lower lip, and I remember how his teeth felt against my mouth. It's still tender. "I'm almost afraid to read your thesis statement."

"I think you'll like it." I rest my hip against the desk. "It's what Dr. Langdon was working on. An aberrant cure. It's been making me think a lot. Since it intersects with your topic…"

"…You killed two birds with one stone." If mention of

Langdon's research jars him, there's no sign. Sighing, he closes the cover and runs his fingers over it. His hands are long and slender, aesthetic. "Do you know when the funeral is?"

I shake my head. "No. I don't even know if his body's been released to his next of kin, or if there's anyone to handle the arrangements. He never talked to me about his family."

"How sad. Eli was always such an angry man."

Eli. So they were on a first-name basis. Something inside me hardens, but I hold my tongue.

"To die in his forties like that…" Trailing off, Sean sets his jaw. That moment of human connection, of what he likely assumes to be shared loss, is over. "If that's all you wanted, Tobias, I'll grade your thesis before finals. Thank you."

"That's not all I wanted."

Standing and shouldering his satchel, he spares a thin, professional smile, then turns away. "If you need help reviewing for finals, my office hours tomorrow are from eight to noon."

"Sean. Stop it." I grip his arm and pull him back around to face me. He may be tall, but I'm stronger than I look. "Come out with me tonight. Dinner. A movie. Something."

"Don't." He jerks free and retreats a step. "The last thing I need right now is someone playing games with me."

"No games. I know—I *know* I kissed you and walked away. I wasn't trying to screw with you. I'd forgotten I had to be somewhere because I…I was enjoying spending time with you." I shrug with a rueful smile. "I'd have called to explain, but I don't have your number."

He gives me a flat look. "It's in the faculty directory."

"And I'm an idiot for not thinking of that." When I take his hand, he doesn't pull away. That's something. "I'm an ass. I admit it. Let me make it up to you."

Sean eyes me, but I can tell he's considering it. "You say you don't want to be my rebound, but now you're asking me out?"

"I don't want to be your rebound, but I do want to take you out. The two don't have to be related."

He quirks a brow. "They can't always be separated."

"Say yes."

With a dirty look, he pulls on his hand. "No."

I tighten my grip and draw him closer. When the tips of my fingers touch his mouth, he inhales gently, lips parting. They're soft to my touch, tender, reddened, a reminder of that ferocious kiss. His lips tremble as I trace their shape—and *I* tremble with the sudden hard thrust of desire spearing deep into my belly, and wonder if I'm pretending at all when I want him, deep and hard.

"Say. Yes," I growl.

His hand grips mine convulsively. His cheeks flush. He starts to speak, stops, then rolls his eyes with an exasperated sound. "Somehow, you keep convincing me to do things against my better judgment."

"Is that a yes?"

He groans. "Yes. *Yes*, you arse. You're horrid. Where are we going?"

"Just wait." I grin. "You'll see."

If you ask a tourist, the best view of Berkeley is from the Claremont Hotel, or the Berkeley Fire Trails. But if you ask a tourist, they'd be wrong.

The best view is from the outdoor plaza of the Lawrence Hall of Science, right there on the UC Berkeley campus. It's an octagonal plaza of stone tiles in dark and light colors, centered by a glimmering, glowing blue fountain and looking out over buildings, parking lots, rolling green slopes of tree-dotted hills stretching down to city streets. I lead Sean across the plaza to the edge, past the sunken model of a fin whale, walking hand in hand in the whipping winds. Sean looks about, lingering on the sky overhead, washed bright by city lights that, reflecting from the bellies of the clouds, hide the stars and almost eclipse the watery moon.

"Six years I've worked at this university, and I've never been out here," he says. "It's so quiet."

"I like to come here to think."

That's too simple, though. Really, I like how it feels to be alone up here on LHS's hillside perch, so far above everything, but until now I've never really thought to see what unfolds before me.

I draw on his hand. "Look."

He catches his breath, and his fingers tighten in mine. The hidden stars are below, a sea of ebbing and flowing light forming ever-changing constellations. We can see all of Berkeley from here: the wooded trails and hilly slopes, the square black shoulders of the business district, the brilliant nightlife, the quieter patchwork of sleeping suburbs, even the dark gash of Strawberry Canyon. It's a pocket of human life I can cup in my hand, bordered by the velvety dark stretch of the bay, where the moon lies on the water like a white-gold coin.

Right now, someone down there is dying. Someone else is being born. Two people fight down the street from two people making love. Countless tears are falling right in this moment, contrast to laughter that chases the darkness away for just a little bit longer. It's so complex, so confusing, yet...

"It's so much simpler up here," I say. "No black and white. No good or evil. Just life, as beautiful and strange as it is."

He looks at me oddly. "Arrogant and amoral, yet you can appreciate beauty."

I steal a strand of his hair back from the cool, biting wind and brush its tip down his cold-flushed cheek. "I wouldn't be human if I didn't."

"No," he murmurs. He lowers his eyes. Shy, I suppose, but there's a touch of that ever-present sadness, as well. "I suppose you wouldn't."

I could kiss him again. His parted lips and downcast eyes invite it. I *want* to kiss him again, but my doubts hold me back. I'm not here for pleasure—and even now, I search his body language for the lie. It would be the perfect cover, really. A professor of ethics dedicated to teaching students the value of life, while secretly collaborating with Langdon to wipe out an aberrant life-form. Maybe he's the associate Langdon mentioned. Maybe all that fragile emotion is just as much of an act as my antisocial awkwardness. Maybe he suspects me as much as I suspect him.

Maybe we're two players circling each other, not quite realizing we're in the same game.

A clunky little compact car pulls into the lot adjacent to LHS. The driver, a rawboned teenager wearing a total of six ironic Livestrong armbands, gets out and tentatively makes his way across the plaza, raising his voice. "Uh…hello? Delivery for…um…Toby?"

"Tobias," I correct.

Sean and I break apart, hands releasing. The pizza delivery driver hangs back, balancing a large box and two bottles of soda.

Sean laughs. "When did you order pizza?"

"Before class."

"Why you arrogant—!"

I can't remember ever laughing like this, full and light and unrestrained, but at Sean's exasperated look I can't help myself. Even the driver looks amused. I pay for the pizza, tip the driver, and send him on his way. Sean watches me with a small smile, hands on his hips.

"You planned this. Were you so certain I'd say yes?"

"No. But if you'd said no, I'd still be covered for dinner."

"*Arse.*"

We settle on the edge of the octagonal fountain, the pizza box between us. Pepperoni with sausage and cilantro; I didn't know what he'd like and figured simpler was better, and when he tucks in without protest I figure I couldn't have gone wrong. For a time we eat in silence, watching the night pass by below. Quiet. Companionable. It's nice.

I can't quite admit that I wish it were real.

The pizza's half gone by the time we've had our fill. With a deep sigh, Sean lies back along the fountain's wide rim, folding his arms beneath his head. He's a portrait in black and white, the only color the flush to his lips and cheeks, the pale tint to his near-colorless eyes. That little smile is back, relaxed and easy and maddeningly seductive.

"I like this," he says, and glances at me. "But I still don't know what I'm doing up here."

"Talking to me." I close the pizza box and push it aside. Shifting closer to him, I lean on one arm and look down at him. "Letting me get to know you."

"Oh? So now you're interested in getting to know me?"

"You're strange." I shrug. "I find that intriguing."

"That sounds suspiciously like what I said to you."

The collar of his dress shirt is unbuttoned, offering a teasing glimpse of his throat. I reach out and finger the next button. He tilts his head back slightly, his neck gently arched. Tempting me. It's so subtle I don't know if he's even conscious of it, but it tells me all I need to know. I could have him, if I want him. I tug first one button loose, then another, my fingers brushing the sleek slope where his neck meets his shoulder, tracing down to the pronounced articulation of his collarbone. He shivers, barely breathing.

"If I recall, you said you weren't afraid of me…yet." I curl my hand against his throat, gripping lightly. Under my palm, his pulse quickens. "Are you now?"

"Oh, Tobias." He laughs. I feel his Adam's apple move. "It takes more than you to frighten me."

I tense and search his face. *You should be afraid*, I want to tell him. *If you knew the truth, you would be.* I yearn to dig my fingers into his throat and show him. I ache to feel him struggle, burn to make him gasp...and I should get as far away from him as possible, before I hurt him in ways words can never repair.

He touches my lips. Without thinking, I kiss his fingertips. He searches my eyes and curls his fingers against my cheek: warmth to warmth, the sensation of skin against skin fascinating, hypnotizing me.

"So I finally see something," he whispers. "A light in the darkness. But it's such a sad light. I wonder...are you lonely, too?"

Capturing his hand, I kiss his palm and the warm, thin skin on the inside of his wrist. "Maybe I am."

"I was serious. I'm not looking for a rebound. I don't know if I'm looking for anything at all." Sean's fingers slip into my hair, the touch electric. "But tonight..."

I nip his wrist. "Hush. Tonight is just tonight."

Sean smiles. "Exactly," he says, and draws me down to kiss him.

It's slower this time, deeper. He takes his time, luring me in, until our mouths are slick with the taste of each other and a lingering hint of spicy cilantro. When his arms slide around me, guiding me down atop him, I go willingly. He steals my breaths and my thoughts, his hands strong on my hips. The heaviness in my stomach and lightness in my chest twist together into something that leaves me torn and on the verge of breaking. I don't know what this is. I burn, yet it's not entirely lust. I crave something more than the slinking feel of his body against mine.

I want him, and that's when I realize I have far more to fear from him than he does from me.

One kiss turns into a haze of desperate caresses that leave me drunk with the taste of him, high off the sensation of our bodies pressed together and trembling with the chemical reaction of two forces crashing together in an explosive burn. I don't remember standing up. I don't remember getting in my car. I barely remember driving to his apartment; all I remember is the marks of his teeth on my neck and the urgency of his hands pushing my jacket and shirt aside to leave stinging, searing bites over my collarbone and shoulders, bites that make me drive that much faster, reckless on the gas.

I hardly even glimpse his apartment. It's just a flash of color, his hand in mine, the bedroom door pushing open and then keys, glasses, clothing falling everywhere, biting into flesh with each ripping pull, naked skin on naked skin, entwined. His body is damp and hot against mine, the sheets searingly cold when he pushes me down to his bed. I arch off the mattress as he strokes his hand down my body, flicks his fingers over my nipples, traces the arc of my rib cage and then ghosts his lips over my sensitive stomach, making every last muscle contract as I suck my breath in and struggle not to let the electric sparks spiraling through me slip free, arousal threatening to rip control of my power out of my hands and light up the room in a blaze of desire.

I try not to cry out. But when he bites down on the crest of my hip, I nearly whimper, twisting against the sheets. He touches me as if he knows me, all the secret things I never knew I needed. Things that make me arch and moan, things that make me hiss in pain as sweet as the kisses that soothe it away. His nails rake down my inner thighs, leaving scorching lines, coaxing them to part. Pale green eyes watch me with a greedy, fevered lividity, nearly too much to endure without the glasses softening them—as if my every hiss, my every gasp of pain and pleasure, feeds something inside him.

For a moment, as I meet his eyes, something stirs inside me. Something I recognize, in a strange, unsettling kinship. Something that tells me he's holding back, just as I'm holding back; if I let myself go completely, I'll hurt him. A shiver goes through me, a shiver that I won't quite admit is an exciting spark of fear. He is my enemy. Even if he wasn't working with Langdon, his very humanity puts us at odds with each other, and whatever it is he's holding back makes him dangerous, a threat to my life.

And that only makes me want him more, desire spiraling as hot as the flames that fill my memories.

I catch his hands just as they frame my hips, pull them away, and tumble him over onto his back with that long, lean body stretched out beneath me, my thighs straddling his, our cocks pressed together in a sweet rush of shuddering, stroking heat—until I can almost feel our pulses matching in the throbbing caress of skin to skin. He stares up at me with wide eyes for a moment, so beautiful against the dark spill of his hair, his skin so luminously pale, and I can't resist leaning down to kiss him.

Until he pulls his hand free from mine, and stops me by pressing his fingertips to my lips.

"Oh no, Tobias," he murmurs, desire turning that lilting voice into dark velvet. "That's not how this works."

I don't understand. Not until he makes me: with the hard flex of his body, with the sudden rush of the room spinning by as he tangles his legs with mine, traps me against him, uses his greater height and weight to spill me over onto my back, pinned beneath him. I growl, struggle, but he forces my wrists to the bed, captures them in a single hand, and slides his body against mine; a mewl I don't recognize as my own voice spills past my lips as every inch of me comes alight with heightened awareness of the sinewy sleekness pressed against me.

Surrender isn't something I understand—yet he teases it from me, makes me a stranger to myself. His fingers leave aching bruises on my wrists. His touch shapes my body, rolling and teasing at my nipples until I can't breathe, feathering light over the shivering slope of my ribs and waist only to dig in again, marking me, taunting me with this alternating rhythm of pleasure and pain that tosses me back and forth in a helpless sea of sensuality, crackling inside with sparks that I can barely keep leashed when he pushes me to the point of madness.

And when his hand wraps around my cock, when he strokes with a dominating surety that rolls waves of tense, writhing heat through my body, I willingly open myself for him. For the slick, lubed press of his fingers, sliding one at a time inside me and stretching me with terrible, wonderful intimacy, piercing me and leaving me vulnerable in ways I've never let myself be to anyone else. The son of the Lord High General submits to no one.

But I submit to him, as those fingers caress and tease me, twisting inside, making me ready for that moment when he withdraws those long fingers and presses the head of his cock against my throbbing, already-sore entrance. I don't even remember if he stopped to put a condom on. I don't care. All I care about is that taut, gorgeous body hovering over mine, and the way he looks at me. Fierce. Intense. As if he could devour me with a single bite, consume me entirely, and it resonates inside me with an emotion I shouldn't be able to feel.

His hand curls against my throat, pressing over my pulse with a sort of tender control that draws a sweet, melting sigh from my lips. Then he rolls his hips forward, and even as the pain takes me, even as he sears me inside and fills me so completely, I wrap my thighs around his hips and wordlessly beg for more. He gives me everything: slow, deep, allowing me to go at his pace or none at all, tormenting me with stop-and-start thrusts that rip me from myself and destroy everything I thought I knew about what I wanted, leaving in its place no preconceptions, no self-delusions, no lies. Only *sensation*, the raw honest truth of being with him, feeling him inside me. Sweat trickles down my spine and tickles the small of my back.

His name spills from my lips, and I am lost.

Chapter Ten

"I didn't love him," Sean says.

We lie tangled in the sheets, the sweat-dampened fabric binding us together in a clinging cocoon. Sean's shoulder pillows my head, firm muscle so hot it nearly burns my cheek. His hair mingles with mine in an indistinguishable pool of darkness, glistening with a sheen of sweat. His glasses are on the nightstand, leaving his eyes unshielded and pensive.

He lifts a clove cigarette to his lips. The curl of aromatic smoke spirals to the ceiling, pale against the dark, exposed cement of the industrial loft-style apartment. Long fold-out windows let in the night, cool enough to make me shiver. His arm tightens around me, gathering me against his warmth.

"Matt, I mean," he continues after a moment, his voice husky and quiet. My hand rests on his chest, just over the red fingernail marks I managed to leave during the half second I wrested my hands free during round two or three; I don't even remember at this point. I can feel each word rumble through the touch. "I didn't love him; I never do. I suppose it's selfish of me, because it's never losing them that hurts, not really. It's just that I failed again. I was supposed to love them, and I couldn't. Sometimes I think I'm just not capable."

"You're human. All humans are capable of love."

He chuckles. "Even you, oh rational and amoral one?"

"Yes." Yet another lie. It has to be, one I cling to desperately when I can still feel the echoes of something unknown and strange, whispering inside me. "I suppose I am."

Sean makes a thoughtful sound, stretches his arm out, and stubs out the clove in the ashtray on the nightstand. "If you can be amoral and still capable of love, then perhaps aberrants are, as well."

My heart lurches drunkenly. Does he know? Has he known me for what I am from the start, and he's only drawing me out, waiting for me to confess? Did I give myself away with a stray burst of sparks as I strained underneath him, when I've never had to fight so very hard to keep my power in check? Has he just been toying with me the entire time?

Why does the thought *hurt*?

Why does anything hurt at all, when I've worked so hard to deaden everything inside me?

"No," I rasp. "They can't. Aberrants can't feel anything."

"Why not?"

"I told you. Because they're monsters." I can't let him go down this path. But I can't say anymore, either—and so I still his moving lips with a kiss.

A kiss becomes a caress. A caress becomes more. He's rougher, almost desperate, as if this night is all there can be, and he's determined to wrest all he can from it. Maybe I'm just as desperate. I clutch at him, bite at him, take everything he gives and demand more. This is something I cannot have. This is something that was never meant for me.

For these few indulgent moments, as we push each other to the edge and beyond, I can only hold fast until I'm forced to let go.

When we collapse together, panting and sore, he kisses my jaw and nuzzles into my throat. "Say you'll stay," he whispers. "Just for tonight."

I say nothing, only brushing my lips to his brow.

If I don't speak, I don't have to lie.

He seems to take that as assent, for with a smile and a soft sigh, he relaxes. Within minutes he drifts off, his breaths and the beat of his heart melding in counter-rhythm that nearly lulls me to sleep. I don't have that luxury. I can't sleep. I came here for a reason, and it wasn't to lose my objectivity over the soft parting of Sean's lips, or the way his arms feel wrapped around me.

Yet I linger for over an hour, watching how his lashes rest against his cheeks, tracing my fingertips along the dusting of fine hair on the backs of his knuckles. Outside cars honk, people shout and laugh, but inside all is quiet. Inside *I* am quiet, for the first time that I can remember.

Why? I know next to nothing about Sean Archer. Physical intimacy is meaningless. Sex is an illusion of closeness, yet being with him is...different. He's not Jeremy. He's not anyone else. He's strange and maddening and so terribly, terribly human.

And I am a fool.

When I'm certain he's sound asleep, I make myself withdraw, sliding from the bed an inch at a time so as not to disturb him. When I stand, he rolls over and stretches his arm across the warm spot where my body had been. His hair streams across the pillow, fine filaments teased into a shining black banner. My fingers itch to touch.

No. *That's not what I'm here for.* Every minute I spent in Sean's arms was just another step closer to what I truly want. Every time I cried out his name, it was only to convince him that I wanted him. I have to believe that.

I have to.

I slide into boxer briefs and jeans, wincing as sore muscles protest; I can still feel the print of his hands dug into my ass and thighs, and in the morning I'll likely have impressive bruises. The uncarpeted cement floor is frigid beneath my bare feet, occasionally relieved by frayed rugs in ornate patterns, maybe Turkish. I follow the blue and green woven runner down the hall to the living room. The apartment is spacious but simple. One bedroom, one bath, and an open kitchen blending into a massive combination living and dining area. No office. Just a laptop on the coffee table, surrounded by stacks and stacks of papers. Good. That'll make it that much easier to search the place.

The bookshelves are all academic texts and historical literature; nothing concealed between the pages or the covers. The kitchen is spartan and clearly never used. Other than the papers, the coffee table is pristinely empty, not even a condensation ring marring the surface. Sean doesn't strike me as a neat freak. Something feels off. The apartment doesn't feel lived in, like a show house without that personal touch needed to make it a home.

No matter how many cabinets I search or couch cushions I lift, I find nothing even hinting at involvement with Langdon or Senator Cranston. So what the hell is setting my nerves on edge? With a sigh, I sink down on the couch. The knit upholstery is scratchy under my hand. If anyone used this couch often, it would be worn smooth.

Stop being paranoid.

So maybe he's just moved, bought new furniture. Or maybe he made a habit of staying with that Matt guy. Maybe he just buys new furniture regularly. There was a bottle of Zoloft in the bathroom cabinet; it's an antidepressant, but it's also used to treat OCD. Sean could be a germophobe or an obsessive neat freak, always replacing his furniture once he feels it's become contaminated. I've seen worse things from people with compulsions.

Pushing the thought from my mind, I flip his laptop open. A burst of flickering static sparks arcs between the screen and my fingers. I jerk back before I can do any damage, and rein myself in. If I'm discharging erratically, I need to calm down.

I don't really expect anything from the laptop, but either he's careless or he has nothing to hide, because it comes up from sleep mode right to the desktop. Not even a log-in screen. There are only four folders on the desktop, two related to coursework, one a collection of photos of Kowloon Walled City, one full of ebooks on Japanese *ikebana*. Flower arranging. There'd been an arrangement on the nightstand, delicate and lovely and precise, but I'd never thought Sean had—

Focus. I don't need to know these things about him. His interests. His frivolous little hobbies. I check the default documents folder. Nothing. On a hunch I open his browser and, just as I thought, he's let it save his email log-in and password on the faculty intranet.

"Jesus, Sean," I mutter.

Forget espionage. He's asking for identity theft.

In his inbox, there's nothing but unopened invitations to faculty events and a heated argument with the department coordinator about his class scheduling. No Langdon. No Cranston. Nothing about aberrants at all. I can't explain the relief that fills me. I don't want to analyze it too closely. It's premature, anyway. There was no blatant evidence at Langdon's house, either.

As a last precaution, I check the pictures folder for any saved document scans or anything else incriminating. Instead I find photos of Sean. Sean and another man, a clean-cut *GQ* type with shallow blue eyes that make me dislike him instantly. In every picture the other man is in the foreground, Sean overshadowed or off to the side. Sean rarely smiles, though the Ken doll flashes his teeth like a show pony. This must be Matt. I'd like to ruin that vain, handsome face and fry that perfect hair.

Jealous now, Spark?

I have to remember who I am. It's Tobias who's the mask, Tobias's life that's the lie. I can't care about these photos. Not of him and Matt; not of him and a younger man who could be Sean some six or seven years back, slim and pretty and green-eyed, obviously a brother or cousin or some other relative, one who can make Sean's smile light up the way he never does in photos with Matt. I close the laptop and give a cursory glance through the stacks of papers. Student essays and quizzes. Sean isn't involved. He's innocent. If I leave him alone, he won't be pulled into this—and he won't have to die.

My thumb catches on a different texture at the bottom of the stack. Newsprint. Frowning, I tug a section of newspaper out. It's dated Sunday, and folded open on a short article hidden away in the funny news section.

MOTHER NATURE TURNS VIGILANTE, the headline reads, above a pithy little blurb about an aberrant assault and robbery attempt foiled by what the victims described as "a tornado come down clear out of the sky." The article plays it off as a dervish, not uncommon in strong winter winds, but it was enough to force the perpetrators to the ground while the victims, a young couple, escaped.

Strange. I'm missing something, something more than the obvious omission of what the police did with the captured aberrants; we're the best-kept secret in the world, always shooed out of the public eye before terror can strike, relegated to either a problem for *over there* away from the Western world or a funny back-page headline. But no—that's not what I'm missing, though I'll be damned if I know what I *am*. Spontaneous windstorms almost sound like something an aberrant might do—but what aberrant would go out of their way to rescue a human?

And why had Sean saved the article?

He probably hadn't. He'd probably been reading the paper and put it down at that spot, only to forget it when it was buried underneath the pile of coursework. I'm grasping at straws. Looking for an answer to this *itchy* feeling of something off; anything to scratch that itch.

I unfold the newspaper to the front page. XINTHIAN DICTATOR DELIVERS AFRICAN ULTIMATUM. The letters take up half the page. So, too, does the full-color photograph of my father, captured in the midst of a rising firestorm. He stands proud, the jut of his jaw cruel, the set of his shoulders commanding. The black and red latex of his outfit makes a stark contrast against the brilliant orange-gold light. It's Bangkok all over again, the memory cold inside me, only this time Maputo burns. I wonder what the hell he wants in Mozambique.

It's probably just another diversion.

I don't want to know. After folding the newspaper over again, I tuck it back into place and layer the papers over it. I need to get my things and leave. Sean is still asleep when I slip back into the bedroom. I've only been gone a few minutes, but best not to push my luck. I pick up my T-shirt and shrug it on. Sean sighs, his fingers curling against the sheets, gripping tightly. His brows draw together, as if disturbed by some nightmare. I know how he feels.

I don't know what I'm doing when I peel out of my shirt and drop it back to the floor. I should be leaving. I've accomplished my purpose, and have no reason to stay. I don't want him. I don't care about him. Yet I strip, slide back into bed, and settle against his side. He stirs with a questioning mumble.

"Bathroom," I whisper. "Go back to sleep."

I wish I could take my own advice—but I can only lay restless and troubled, watching the arc of moonlight inch its way across the ceiling and wondering at this inescapable feeling of dread.

Eventually, near dawn, I sleep. These late nights are taking their toll, and I'm too exhausted to stay awake. By the time morning wakes me, the bed is empty, the sheets still warm where he slept. I can smell burning eggs. It's like being at home.

Yawning, I shrug into my clothing. The soreness is worse, but it'll fade. I need a shower more than anything. The bruises and bite marks mostly vanish under my T-shirt. My jacket collar will hide the rest, and it's not like I have friends or coworkers to notice. Sean, on the other hand, will have a hell of a time explaining the dark bite standing out like a brand of possession on his pale throat.

Possession. Not a thought I want to linger on.

I pick up my shoes and pad into the living room. Sean looks entirely out of place in the kitchen, prodding awkwardly at a sad mass of half-blackened eggs and melted cheese. He looks up with a sheepish smile.

"Sorry. I'm not much of a cook. I didn't wake you, did I?"

"No. I'm used to waking up around this time for morning classes."

He's still disheveled, walking about barefoot in boxers and a half-buttoned shirt, his hair wild. I can't help myself; I slide my arms around him from behind and press a kiss to his shoulder.

"I have to go or I'll be late," I murmur.

He turns the stove off and looks at me over his shoulder.

"Promise me you'll get something to eat on the way."

I realize he doesn't want me to go. Whatever last night was about, sex was only part of it. Warning shrills its cold touch up and down my spine. This man is vulnerable, emotionally damaged, and I could crush him with a word.

Just like my father: I find something beautiful, use it for my own ends, then destroy it.

I hesitate a moment, then smile and tighten my grip, pulling him against me. "I will. Thanks. I'll see you later."

"Tobias." He turns in my arms, facing me. "It's all right to say it. I know we can't do this again." His one-sided smile is wistful, resigned. "Last night was just last night."

I reach up to finger the collar of his shirt. It gives me something to look at so I don't have to meet his eyes. "I know. I just didn't want to hurt you."

He laughs, resting his hand on my chest. "I told you—don't say it if you don't mean it."

"I do."

His laughter stills. His brows furrow. He tilts his head to the side, studying me. "You know, I almost believe you."

"Amoral," I murmur. "Not heartless."

I steal a lingering kiss. His mouth is soft against mine, his breaths sighing and slow. I weave my fingers into his hair, hands stroking through the luxurious tangle, taking my fill of him. For once he's pliant and giving, and I can taste his pain in every touch of his lips. He's too proud to say anything, and too afraid. This is the last time. The only time.

It has to be.

I break back with a gentle nip to his upper lip. "I'll see you in class Wednesday."

"Sure," he says, and wraps his arms around himself. "Try to stay awake this time."

The words feel like everything except what we really want to say.

After letting myself out into the thin morning light, I head home to change and feed Samadhi before class. I don't understand this gnawing feeling in my chest. It's done. I learned what I came to learn. It's nothing more than that. It can't be.

For Sean's own safety, this can't happen again.

It happens again.

After my morning Genetic Epidemiology class, I run into him at the student center. He's coming out the wide glass double doors just as I'm coming up the steps. We freeze at the same time—him still gripping the door, me with my foot on the top step and my hand on the rail, both of us staring. No way around each other; no way to breeze past and pretend we didn't see each other. I'm surprised by the sudden bands of iron that clamp down on my heart and stomach and squeeze simultaneously; I'm not ready for this, when I'd thought I'd have until Wednesday to put the numbing filter of distance between me and him.

He breaks the silence first. "Mr. Rutherford." Back to my formal name; back to that strained, polite smile that doesn't quite reach his eyes. "Good morning. Fancy seeing you here."

I rise to the top step and slide my hands into my pockets, shrugging with more casualness than I really feel. "A student and a teacher, both on campus at the same time. The odds are staggering."

He blinks, then laughs; this time that laugh reaches his eyes, and his stiff shoulders lower. "Oh come off it, you sarcastic berk." With an amused sound, he wraps his arms around himself. "You must admit, this is awkward."

"Would it have been any less awkward in class, with everyone watching?"

"I can't say I'm much of an exhibitionist."

If I didn't expect that vise around my heart, I'm doubly thrown by the sudden hard, cold stab of possessive, almost furious jealousy. In my mind's eye, I can see him on performance—for the class, for a dozen others, for men like that smiling Ken doll who look at him with a sort of greed that leaves him nearly slimed with their touch, coating his skin.

I don't like it.

I bite back a growl, watching him intently. "You're a lot of things," I say. "But no. Not that."

He stares at me; color etches the outlines of his cheekbones into stark relief. "Tobias…"

I don't know what to say to the soft entreaty in his voice. And I can't look at him like this, or I'll remember his body arched over mine. I'll remember the way his arm curled around me, and the way he looked so *content* falling asleep tangled up with me, like we both actually belonged there.

I look away, curling my fists in the pockets of my coat. "You've been all right?"

"Did you expect I wouldn't be?" he asks a touch archly.

"That's not an answer."

"I'm fine." When I say nothing, he sighs. "I *am*. It was what it was."

Still I say nothing, but I fix him with a skeptical glance. He tilts his head quizzically, then laughs, incredulous and sweet, and shakes his head.

"Oh, get *over* yourself." He smirks. His gaze rakes me. "I should be asking if you're all right."

"Why wouldn't I be?"

"That's not an answer, either."

"I know that." And I'm not giving him a real answer. Not when I'm *not* all right. I'm not, I should be, and it's tearing at me to feel so right and so *wrong* with him close by and the taste of his body still on my lips. "I'm sore," I deflect.

"That's satisfying."

Something close to a purr enters his voice. Husky, dark, and I remember that same dark, rough-edged burr as he dug his fingers into my wrists and held me down and whispered my name. The lingering bruises throb in tribute, in memory, in longing, and I scowl.

"You're smug."

He inclines his head with no argument, his eyes glittering. "I'm free for the rest of the afternoon."

My pulse picks up. "Is that an invitation?"

"Just a statement of fact."

But in that statement of fact is a question. A *compulsion*. A need to make last night happen again. And again and again and again, and to tell myself over and over again it's just physical, just an answer to the pull he has on my body. Need is ravenous inside me: a beast unleashed and craving, threatening to devour me if I don't give it what it wants.

Him. Him, and the things he does to me that no one else has dared.

Just physical, I tell myself, as I step closer to him. "I still haven't eaten."

"There's food at my apartment," he answers softly, and I draw closer still. As close as I dare, when we're a student and teacher in public in the light of day, trading in darklings that belong in the shadows.

"Are you offering?"

Heat darkens his eyes. He leans toward me: subtly, but there, as if some invisible leash barely binds him in place. "I'm offering."

"Then why are we still here?"

Somehow I end up on the back of his motorcycle — and back in his bed. Somehow I end up pinned beneath him, and spreading my legs until my thighs ache and burn and I'll do anything for him to fill the void inside me, anything for him to ease the almost painful sensitivity making me flinch every time his fingers, his lips, his tongue brush my cock. He makes me beg. He leaves me blind, sparks filling my vision. We envelop each other, a twist of limbs and sinew and desire, and his hair pools against my chest in icy slithers that sear my skin with a cold burn as he moves over me with his lips parted slack and that fixed intensity consuming his features.

This can only be body to body, lust to lust, this all-encompassing fire just the fascination of something new, something different. We are alien creatures to each other, and that makes every moment one of hypnotized discovery, wonder, awe. It's only the newness of it, I tell myself—even as I pull him deeper into me, clench my thighs against his hips, tug and pull at his hair. That's all. That's *all*.

That's all I'll let it be.

It's hours before we wear each other out and tumble into the sheets to languish for the rest of the afternoon. With Langdon's lab closed, my day is free, and Sean's lecture isn't until evening. We don't talk. I think I'm afraid to, when my heart is beating too hard in my chest and my head is full of things I can't name, but they hurt in a strangely wondrous way. I tell myself I'll leave when he goes to his lecture, but by then I've dozed off. I don't wake until he's already back and dropping his satchel on the couch. He kisses me, trailing his fingers down my chest.

By the time his shirt comes off, there's no point in going anywhere.

Over an hour later, we draw the damp covers around us. "I read your thesis," he says. His fingers toy through my hair. "The hawk and the sparrow. I liked it."

Ah. That thing. *Every life-form on earth is a mutation of another*, I'd written. *The hawk and the sparrow are both mutated offshoots of a common ancestor. We don't kill the hawk for being a different bird from the sparrow, though one is stronger and preys on the other. Yet we kill aberrants for being different from humans although they, too, are men, born of a common ancestor. Such hypocrisy is intolerable and unethical in the face of the basic right to life.*

Sean cups my cheek. "Did you mean it, or were you pandering for a good grade?"

"If I were pandering for a good grade, I'd have started sleeping with you earlier."

He smacks my chest. "I'm serious."

Laughing, I catch his hand and kiss his knuckles. "I don't know, honestly. Theory is all well and good, but it's different when you're the sparrow. Still." I sigh. "Maybe if we stopped killing them, they'd stop killing us."

"Maybe." He smiles. His eyes crease at the corners when he does. "You aren't as horrid as you pretend, Tobias. Not at all."

But I am.

I just don't know how to make him see it in a way that won't destroy him.

Chapter Eleven

When we part ways again, I tell myself it's the last time.

I say the same thing the next night.

And the next.

His apartment is starting to feel too comfortable. At night we lay together, catching our breath, while he tells me things I shouldn't know, things I shouldn't care about. He tells me about Clovelly. He tells me of the high cobbled streets, of swimming in the ocean at Blackchurch Rock, of exploring the old stone abbey. In return, I tell him about Thailand before the conquest. I tell him of visiting the Wat Pho temple with my mother, of laying orchids before the Reclining Buddha, of the scent of jasmine that clung to everything, and of how the monsoons come and stay until everything is wet and the rain becomes a part of your pulse—and of how when it finally leaves, you find you can't sleep without its steady, drumming sigh.

I give him pieces of myself, as if only his hands can arrange the puzzle of them into something human.

"Do you miss it?" he asks. He leans over me, a naked

sylph with his hair tumbling over him.

"Yes. Maybe more because it's gone, and I can never go back."

I don't realize how true it is until the words are past my lips. When I was a boy, I grew up surrounded by people who looked like me. People for whom being brown and lithe and dark-eyed and beautiful was *normal*, instead of *other, lesser*. Those people are still in Xinth, buried among the massive influx of aberrants of every color and culture from around the world. It's those buried people who remember that jasmine scent and the sound of the monsoons. A scent, a sound very few here at the university would know, or care about. If they did, it would just be another thing that would let them call me *exotic*, like I'm some kind of zoo animal or imported food. The bits and pieces of my life, my *self*, packaged up into consumer commodities, bite-sized bits of quaint little entertainment in the form of cultural curiosities.

Once, I thought I knew what it was like to be normal— and it had nothing to do with being aberrant or not, and everything to do with being accepted by people for whom my *oddities* were nothing but part of their every day.

I'm homesick. I'm homesick for a place my father destroyed, and that I can never rebuild.

I wonder if the ever-exalted Lord High General still remembers how to speak Thai, or if he forgot after my mother died. I wonder, too, if Sean would care if I wanted to teach him.

Just to hear my mother tongue from someone else's lips.

Sean's gaze flicks back and forth searchingly, fixed on me thoughtfully. "You're somewhere else right now," he whispers. "Somewhere heavy, and dark."

"Am I?" I smile faintly and shift to adjust the pillows under my head. "If nostalgia and regret are a place, I guess that's where I am."

"Be careful, Mr. Rutherford. Those sound like suspiciously

moral emotions for the Grand Philosopher."

"Shut *up*." With a laugh, I shove at his chest. He laughs as well, and sprawls out at my side, resting on his stomach with his cheek pillowed on his folded forearms. Pale green eyes watch me over the hard cut of his forearm like a crocodile peering above the water.

"What are you thinking about?"

I groan. "That question is the death of every relationship."

"Are we in a relationship, now?"

I still. Fuck, I wish my stomach wouldn't do that *thing* when he asks me questions like that—like I've swallowed a thousand needles and they're darting holes in me from the inside. "We're doing a thing."

"A thing?"

"Does it need a name?"

"I wouldn't mind calling it The Grand Sexing. It sounds much more glamorous than a relationship."

Only then do I realize by the merry glimmer in his eyes that he's teasing me. The bastard is *teasing* me. I want to feel relieved that he isn't pushing this, that he isn't trying to make it *more* than I can give him: a few nights of sex, a little idle company. But all I can do is growl, scowling at him and snagging the pillow to *whump* it at his head.

"I hate you. Fiercely and unapologetically."

Chuckling, he rolls onto his back, snagging the pillow and yanking it from my grip to hug against his chest. "No, you don't. But you probably should, considering how much I enjoyed the sheer bloody *terror* in your eyes."

"Hate."

"If you'd like, I can remind you why you don't."

"If you touch me, you'll pull back a stub. I need to be able to *walk* in the morning."

His delighted laughter fills the room again, ringing out soft and low until I can't help but smile myself, watching how his face lights up and his shoulders tighten with every slightly raspy snicker. I don't even realize time is passing, caught in this strange place where the curve of his lips and the rise and fall of his chest becomes my entire world, but I shake myself as he quiets with a heavy, almost whistling sigh, relaxing against the bed.

"Ah, Tobias." His head falls to one side, toward me; his eyes are half-lidded, soft. "You're so different from anyone else I've ever been with."

My smile disappears. It's like that every time—every casual, innocuous moment that could mean I've given myself away, and the needles are back in my stomach again. "Different?"

"Mm. I don't know how to explain it. Like you see the world through different eyes."

I shift to look at the ceiling, rather than at him, folding my arms beneath my head. "Maybe I do."

"Hazard of not being born here?"

"Maybe. But you weren't, either."

"Yes, but…"

He trails off with an uncomfortable sound. And maybe it's how isolated I feel, maybe it's how raw I am remembering the ferries on Khlong Saen Saeb and the fluttering banners stretched over Arab Street, but when I realize what he means it hits just close enough to home to gut me.

When I realize that he means *I'm white, and you're not.*

I don't want to be angry. I know it's more about culture shock. About how much easier it is to go from one English-speaking country to its bastard offspring, rather than the complete one-eighty it is for me. I *know* he doesn't mean anything by it, but right now he's such an easy target for my anger and frustration and loneliness—when he's the very thing that makes me lonely for something I can never have.

"Don't. Don't go there." I push myself up, my teeth

pressing hard against the inside of my lips as I clench them, glaring at him. "What am I to you? Just some exotic indulgence? You see my skin, my accent, and you want to try something different?"

"No. No, I—" The dumbstruck look on his face is at once gratifying and terrible. Moving slowly as a man walking through a minefield, he pushes himself up, setting the pillow aside; the sheets bunch around his waist. "Have...have I treated you that way?"

Yes, I want to snarl, but I can't lie just to make him hurt the way I'm hurting. I don't *understand* this. I turn away from him, sliding my legs out to sit on the edge of the bed, my back to him. It's the only way I can answer honestly. The only way I can get past that urge to crush something beautiful and say:

"No."

Silence. I can feel his helplessness like a presence in the room. "Tobias...am I doing something wrong?" he asks my back. "Have...have I been ignoring something important?"

"No. It's more that I've been suppressing it."

"Don't." The sound of sheets hissing and whispering, a shift of the mattress...and then he presses against my back, all solid heat and comforting pressure and strong hands against my shoulders, the fall of his hair tumbling over me in cool liquid washes, his voice a rumble against my back. "Don't suppress who you are."

Don't, I tell myself, but I close my eyes, leaning back into him. "I have to."

"Not with me."

"Even with you." I tilt my head back against his shoulder, closing my eyes. "Especially with you."

"Tobias?"

"I've...I've never..."

His grip tightens. "Never...?"

I swallow back the block in my throat. "I've never been

with someone like you."

His silence says he doesn't understand. I'm not sure I do, either. Because I'm not sure what I'm thinking. *I've never been with a human.* Not like this. I was never *with* Kalen. Just using him. Using him for easy cover, using him for his pretty dark skin and plush round lips. I wasn't *here* with him. Not like I am with Sean.

"Have…you never…" Sean fumbles. "Have you never been with a white man?"

I almost want to laugh at how tentatively he says it. How he stumbles around like he's questioning, with every word, what he's *allowed* to say. It's almost sweet, how he doesn't want to misstep. How he's trying so hard to be sensitive to what I'm going through, and yet he's so far off the mark while still being so very close.

"Yeah," I lie. It's easier. Jeremy probably doesn't count, anyway, when Jeremy is barely more than a blow-up doll that talks, and his subservience never made me wonder if the man holding me so close saw me as his equal, or as an exotic amusement.

I'm so fucked up right now. Telling him the truth and lying at the same time. Masking what I can't tell him behind what I can.

I'm an aberrant, Sean. I'm an aberrant and I can never tell you, and I feel alien in so many fucking ways when even people who think I'm human see me as inferior just for being brown.

You can't comfort that.

You can't fix any of it.

He remains quiet against my back, the only sound his heart beating against my shoulder blade, its steady rhythm soothing me. There's a waiting tension between us, a question he wants to ask, and I wait him out until he speaks.

"Is that a deal-breaker?" he asks softly.

"It's just…it puts me on edge." I shake my head. "You

wouldn't understand."

"Of *course* I can't understand!" he flares, sudden and hot, before taking a trembling breath and pressing his brow to the nape of my neck, his breaths curling down my spine. "I know that. I know it's not the same. I won't insult you by pretending it is. But even if I can't understand, I can listen." His hold on me tightens. "I can give you room to breathe."

I pull away so I can shift to face him. There's something so earnest in his eyes, something so desperate. As if there's some pain inside him that's bleeding, and he's trying to hold it all in so it won't spill out and stain me. I want to tell him, so much. I want to tell him the truth and hope this stupid, overly emotional human will understand, will have enough compassion and empathy to care, to want, to offer me…I don't know.

I've never thought about looking for forgiveness before.

And I can't think about it now.

I shake my head and reach for his hand, curling it in my own. "Have I ever told you about Visakha Puja?"

He looks puzzled, but his hand clings almost desperately to mine as he shakes his head. "No. What is Vee… Vee-shak…"

"Visakha Puja," I correct softly. That smile is back on my lips, and I don't really know why. I shift to lie against the headboard and draw him against me—laying his head to my chest, holding him for once instead of the other way around, feeling how he fits into my arms and the way his body takes up space against me and inside me. "It's a Buddhist holiday. I…I'd like…you to know, I suppose. About things like that. About…my normal."

He rubs his cheek against my chest, draping his arm across my stomach. "You want it to be my normal, too."

"Yeah. Something like that."

I feel his smile against my skin. "Then tell me," he says. "I want to hear about it. All about your…" A pause, and then he pronounces very carefully, "Vi-sak-ha Pu-ja."

"Stupid," I murmur, and press my lips into his hair. "But close enough."

With a chuckle, he relaxes against me — and I tell him. I tell him about Visakha Puja, about how it celebrates the life and enlightenment and death of Buddha. Of my mother cleaning the house madly every May in preparation, and the scent of flickering candles from the household shrine. Of the visits to the churches to give alms, and how my mother would let me carry the donations in my tiny chubby hands and lift me up so I could reach the coffers. Of how my father would always try to read from the Four Noble Truths and would never get it right, and my mother would always have to translate for him and they'd laugh together and that was when we'd felt like a family, in that moment when it seemed as if the Buddha was watching us and holding us together against a storm we didn't yet know was coming.

Every word past my lips relaxes me — and I feel Sean go soft in my arms, quiet and still, but when I look down at him he's watching me intently, as if he really cares. As if he really wants to understand, to know these parts of me that make me whole, that would change how I thought about life and love and family if I had a chance to be human.

If, I think, and wonder if it's possible to just…give it all up, and pretend to be what I'm not forever.

"I'm a terrible Buddhist, honestly," I say, and idly walk my fingers down his arm. "I know it, but I don't live it. It feels like it stopped meaning anything after she died, and now it's just backdrop. I suppose I've become Americanized. I don't think about it. I don't think about the things that shaped me, because I'm too busy living the day to day."

"Is that really all it is?" he asks.

My brows knit. "What do you mean?"

"You talk about these memories of your mother with

love." *Do I?* "You said that Visakha Puja is about family. Then you lost the woman who gave you a sense of family… Wouldn't it feel like Buddhism betrayed you, in a way?"

"Mm. Maybe. I don't know. It's about letting go, in a lot of ways. Shedding yourself of the things that…well, that fuck up your life and your peace." I laugh, and it tastes bitter. "Maybe that's why when I came here, I let go of who I am. Nothing fucks up my life and my peace more than I do." I trail off, looking up at the ceiling but not really focusing on more than the haze of dark, gritty stone and the shadowed cones of hanging lampshades. "No…I let go long before. Just lately I've started thinking about finding that again. I've started wondering just how close the walls of my box really are, and wondering if I can stand to push the boundaries."

Sean's hand settles to rest over my heart. "Why don't you?"

"It's complicated."

"Is it? And don't give me any bollocks about how I wouldn't understand. You only get to use that cop-out twice."

"What's my count now?"

"Six."

I narrow my eyes. "It is not. Are you really counting?"

"No, but the fact that you had to ask says you know six isn't that far off." With a sigh, he props his chin on my chest, cushioned on the back of his hand. "You're not the only one who ran away from home, you know. I left behind my parents, my younger brother…" He smiles faintly. "A goat farm. A *goat* farm, Tobias."

"That explains the smell."

"Oh, come off it."

I chuckle. "Why'd you run away, then, farm boy? Don't you miss your goats?"

"*Yes*, I do, thank you very much. Goats are cute, you sod." He snorts, eyes half-closing, contemplative and quiet. "If you'd asked me years ago, I'd have said I left because I wanted something better. For myself, and for my family. Mayhap I had these grand ideas of making something better for myself, and coming back a changed man who would be able to make their lives easier instead of harder."

I finger a lock of his hair, coiling it around my knuckle. "What did you do to make their lives so hard?"

No answer. And for a moment I don't think he even sees me, that maddening little smile of his fading, his expression blank. And when something finally does cross his features, I don't know how to read it. I don't know what it is.

All I know is that he might as well have told me he was about to lie.

"Ambition," he says a little too flatly. "Ambition is expensive, you know. I worked my way through uni but barely made enough for living expenses. I was arrogant and young and wanted to be *away*, because I thought *away* meant better. But while I was busy being away, they were giving up their meager savings to pay for my tuition. And while it's not as beastly expensive as it is here in the States…"

It's not wholly a lie, I think. The regret is too real. But it's masking something else, even if the ache in his voice is all too true, too deep, his eyes glimmering faintly, wetly.

"I feel like I took everything from them. From my brother, too. Keane." He smiles, but it's tremulous and hurt. "And I paid back every pence and pound, in spades. I'm paying Keane's university tuition right now, but I can't ever forget how they struggled for what they gave up for me. And I feel like I don't deserve to go home, because of what I took from them."

He's so *intense*. How can he stand to live with such intensity of emotion? How does he not drown in it, in himself, every day?

I push myself up to kiss him. It's the only way I know how to offer comfort. With touch, with intimacy, with *presence*.

"You think they resent you," I murmur, and he lets out a choked, wet-sounding laugh against my lips.

"How can they not?"

"Just because you resent yourself doesn't mean they resent you." I curl my fingers in his hair, stroke against the back of his neck. "Other people rarely see us the way we see ourselves. Other people rarely hate us the way we hate ourselves."

He leans hard into me, almost desperately. "Do you hate yourself, Tobias?"

"Every day."

"Why?" He makes a rough sound. "No—don't tell me. I wouldn't understand."

"No more than I can really understand you." I rest my brow to his. "It's a lonely life, not being understood."

"A lonely life, for lonely people." He trails into a near whimper that tears at me to hear, with a force I'm unaccustomed to feeling—as if he'd stabbed me with that sound, drenched my heart in his emotions. "Am I allowed to hate it when I *chose* this?"

"Yes," I whisper, and take him fiercely into my arms. Because this, I understand. This choice to be alone, because solitude is safer and yet so very, very terrible. "*Yes*."

He burrows into me, making an oddly small bundle for such a large man.

"You aren't the only one running from something," he mumbles against my skin. "You aren't."

"I know." I close my eyes and curl around him and cradle him close. "And you aren't the only one who's lonely. So for as long as we can...let's be lonely together. Until we have to run again."

"Until?"

"Until," I answer. It's inevitable. It has to be.

He only holds me tighter, and says nothing else as we drift

off in a painful and yet strangely intimate silence.

He asks nothing of me the following morning. Not that I come the next night, or stay a little longer; not that I take him out to dinner or meet his friends, if he even has any; not that I define this thing between us, or be anything to him. I keep my silence as well. It is what it is.

I don't know how to let it be anything else.

The week before finals passes in a haze of Sean, studying, too little sleep, and too many emails from Jeremy. New plans. New identities. New travel itineraries. Langdon's emails have changed everything, and for once my father and I are in agreement. New Hampshire is out of the question. Too little, too late. If we act quickly and move on D.C., Dad's plans will position me to put Cranston down like the human dog he is, before he can do irreversible damage.

We're cutting it close to the wire, and I'm running out of time. I have trouble caring. Sunday morning, it's all I can do to drag myself out of Sean's bed and trudge home. I have Samadhi to take care of, and I don't want Sean to catch me dealing with my father's business.

When I step into my building, I know immediately that something's wrong. It's a current on the air, a sense of things displaced, that same perception that tells you a stranger's been in your home after a break-in. On my floor, I slip from the staircase into the hall, hand drifting toward the knife I keep in my jacket.

A man stands before my apartment door, his back to me. As he turns, my body goes numb. Breakfast turns heavy in my stomach; for a moment my vision swims, and I can barely speak the single dry, crumbling word on my lips.

"...Dad?"

Chapter Twelve

In a casual suit and tie, stripped of his mantle of command, my father is a rather unimposing man. Michael Cornelius Rutherford is of average height, average build, his dark brown skin smooth, and his strong, angular face just beginning to show lines of age. His tightly curled black hair is cropped close, touched with streaks of advancing gray. He exudes no menace, only a quiet certainty and a particular charismatic strength. Looking at this man, standing before me with his hands laced together and a small frown on his lips, one would never guess what he's capable of.

"Tobias," he says gravely. "It's good to see you."

I stay where I am. He shouldn't be here. The fact that he is tells me there's something very wrong. I don't trust him, and I'm going to kill Jeremy for not warning me. "What are you doing here?"

"Please, let's talk inside." He gestures to my door.

"Sure." I edge past him, careful not to touch him. It's like stepping around a half-buried land mine. After unlocking the door, I step inside and flip on the lights. Samadhi twines around my ankles, but shies away when my father enters. She's edgy around strangers, and in the four years that I've had her, she's seen him only once. I gesture toward the living room. "Have a seat."

He settles into my easy chair, crossing his legs. He has the solemn bearing of a king, and suddenly this apartment doesn't feel like my home anymore. It's just an extension of his domain.

"Another human, Tobias?" he asks without preamble. "Another *white* human?"

I lean against the wall next to the door. "How long have you been watching?"

"Jeremy's been here for two days."

"So now you're spying on me?"

His brows lower. "You're behaving erratically. I need to know I can trust you. You are my right hand—"

"Except I'm not. That's Jeremy. You trust him more than you trust me. I'm not your right hand. I'm just the blunt object you beat people with." I shove away from the wall and head for my bedroom. I need to shower and change. Sean's scent clings to me, and for some reason I don't want my father to catch even a whiff of him. It's bad enough that he's human. I don't even know how to start unraveling the racial issues that make my father mistrustful, that sometimes even give me pause and make me wonder what Sean really sees when he looks at me. Over my shoulder, I bite off, "If you're worried about Washington, don't be. I know my place. Cranston will have an accident, and his plans die with him. Just like Langdon."

"That's another thing," he says, and I stop. "The plan has changed. I didn't feel safe using traceable communications, and felt it best to tell you in person. That, and…" He hesitates. "I've missed you, son."

Pretend sentimentality. I learned it from him, that false

mask of human emotion that lets us blend in. "Don't say it if you don't mean it," I say, and walk away.

I hope, by the time I finish showering and dressing, he'll be gone—but I know him better than that. When I shrug into a fresh shirt and jeans and step into the living room, he's still in my chair, Samadhi on his lap. Little traitor.

"I'm staying in the San Francisco Marriott Marquis," he says. "Jeremy and Alice are with me. They'll be staying behind to accompany you. I'll be flying out tomorrow."

Alice. I'm not surprised he chose her. She's the model of obedience, a point-and-shoot weapon who'll kill on command. One of the few who've been with Xinth since infancy, incapable of questioning my father's righteous cause. He took Alice from her parents, slaughtering them in the maternity wing of a Seattle hospital. He'd done the same to many young couples over the years, anyone unfortunate enough to birth an aberrant child—"rescuing" children before human society could get their hands on them. He told me to think of all these wayward children as my brothers and sisters.

As if he could replace my mother. As if anyone could.

I frown. "I don't need backup. They'll get in my way."

"As I said, the plan has changed. You're not to assassinate Cranston. Sit down."

And so I sit. And so he speaks. And when he tells me the plan, I realize it's more than a show of force. It's a declaration of war, and my father doesn't believe in a bloodless coup. I've always known he's quite mad, brilliantly so. I never thought he'd destroy the very foundation of the United States government.

And I never thought he'd command me to murder Congress.

He might as well have told me to kill the president.

By the time he leaves, I have everything I need to get three people into the Capitol building unseen—except the guts to do it. It had been a matter of self-preservation when it was only one man, but this? This could trigger all-out war.

If there's anyone left to lead it.

I sink down on the couch, staring at the television without really seeing it. This should be easy. I wiped out half the population of Laos. Three million people. A few hundred senators and state representatives should be nothing, but I know what will happen after.

The United States won't submit calmly. Neither will my father. One properly trained aberrant is as effective as a thousand human soldiers, even with sophisticated weaponry. A nation of aberrants could take on the U.S. Armed Forces, but they'll call in allies. I don't know who'd win. I do know it wouldn't end until either every last aberrant was dead, or there was nothing left of the three hundred million people of this nation but slaves or corpses.

Including Sean.

I hate that he comes to mind now. I hate that I care. The first night we slept together, I had been willing to kill him if he became a problem. I think. I don't know. I don't know anything anymore. I don't know what to do if I don't follow my orders.

If I'm not my father's shadow, there's nothing else for me. Without his leash around my neck, I'm nothing but a rabid dog let loose. I may loathe what he stands for, but I can't deny that his structure, his order, are the only things keeping me in check and letting me maintain this illusion of human sanity.

I want to break something, but Jeremy's probably watching me even now, reporting on my every move. Visible anger will only raise more doubts and bring my father back. I want to go to Sean and tell him everything. Take him and run away. My father won't let us go, but I can protect us. I can stop this from happening. I was trained to fight.

It's about time I used it for something worthwhile.

No. I shouldn't be having these thoughts. They're irrational, ridiculous, impossible. I am an aberrant. A deviant. My mind is as warped as my powers, and these things I feel...they're not possible. Not real. It's an illusion. Part of my psychosis. It has to be.

I can't let it be anything else.

For the next week, I avoid Sean. It's not hard, yet it's one of the hardest things I've ever done when my bed feels too large, empty and cold, and his touch is an addiction I can't shake. I find myself missing the strangest things, like the taste of the brand of toothpaste he uses or the way my arm goes numb after hours sandwiched against him. But I have exams to take, internship applications to file, next semester's courses to plan. He's busy with testing, with grading, with frantic students who can't believe, after a semester of slacking, that they're going to fail. He looks tired when I sit for his exam. When I catch his eye, he manages a brief smile. He doesn't suspect anything wrong. No strings. Right.

The night of my exam, I consider dropping by his place — but a glimpse of motion overhead stops me before I can even get into my car. Jeremy. He's just a dark irregularity on the roof of my building, but I know him. I know he'll follow me. I can't go to Sean. Instead I drive to the bay, and the rocky slope on Eastshore Freeway where we first kissed. Alone it's colder, darker, but it gives me space to think. Less than a week.

Less than a week before it all crashes down, and I lead the descent into global war.

Christmas Eve is the day. Cranston's called a special joint session of Congress to present what he calls his "gift to the world." That's when Dad wants to do it. It'll be nationally televised. People will be home with their families, their friends, waiting to share the next day with their loved ones. I don't remember what it's like, but I know how quickly it can be taken away. They'll watch, glued to the television, as I destroy the foundation that makes them feel secure in their bright, normal human lives.

My flight's scheduled for Sunday. Saturday afternoon I leave Samadhi with a pet boarder, paid in advance, with a note to call Sean if I'm not back by the second week of January. I can't explain this to Sean, but I know he'll make sure she goes to a good home if I don't come back. There's a very good chance I won't.

I don't sleep that night. I can't. My things are packed: a few changes of clothing, my laptop, my gear and weapons—which shouldn't be hard to sneak through airport security with Jeremy's help. There's nothing in the apartment I'm really attached to. It's all just the trappings of a false life. Everything that mattered burned in Thailand, nearly sixteen years ago. All my memories.

All my humanity.

I can't take it anymore. It's almost three a.m., but I have to see Sean one last time. He doesn't have to know. As long as he doesn't see me, I don't have to say goodbye.

I slip out onto the fire escape. No car. I don't want to be part of the human world. Not tonight. I'm just a shadow, and soon enough I'll fade away.

As I reach the roof, another shadow intercepts me. Jeremy steps into my path. He's masked, sheathed in slick latex, black trimmed in orange—but I know him. I know his smile, courteous and chilly.

"Young Master," he says. I could only get him to stop calling me that when he was straining beneath me, calling me a bastard, begging for more. "Stepping out for the night?"

"Personal business. I'd suggest you let it stay personal."

"I'm afraid I can't do that."

I study him. There's a charged, prickling tension between us, latent and ready to snap. Without a word I elbow past him, but he places himself in my path again, cool, implacable.

"You're making a mistake, Tobias." His fingers trace over my shoulder. "Trust me. I'm only looking out for your best interests."

My hand snaps out and wraps around his throat. He stiffens and scrabbles at my fingers, sucking in a sharp breath. He doesn't dare fight too hard, or use his power against me. My motives may be suspect, but I am still Spark. He knows, too, that I could kill him before he can draw another breath. He can change the fundamental state of matter without heating or cooling—solidify air, liquefy stone, vaporize water—but I can change the nature of atoms themselves. Electrical ionization. Ionize the atoms in the human body, and the molecules of every cell fall apart or twist themselves into horrific new configurations that could never be human again. Jeremy has a little more trouble working with the complex components of the human body.

The extra seconds are all I would need to leave him a wreck of broken flesh at my feet.

I tighten my grip. I want to do it. I want to hear him scream. I've been holding myself back with Sean for weeks, struggling not to hurt him, and that *urge* is a living thing inside me, hungry and desperate to be fed. The power crackles in my fingertips, responding to my desire. Only the high neck of his suit protects him; latex is an insulator. Rip it away, and I could destroy him.

"Tomorrow," I hiss, "I'm yours. I'll do what he wants. I'll fight for him. Kill for him. I'll be his weapon, wholly and willingly, and he'll never doubt me again. But tonight I belong to myself. Follow me, and you'll be the first to go."

He tries to speak and chokes, gasping. I loosen my grip just enough to let him rasp, "It doesn't matter. Your human will die with the rest."

For that, I curl my fingers just inside the neck of his suit and let loose a sharp surge, sharp enough that for just a moment his flesh turns translucent as electricity crackles through in a collar of bright-stinging thorns around his throat. He screams, and it's one of the most satisfying things I've heard in a long time. Satisfying enough that I can let him go, dropping him without a second thought.

I leave him sprawled on the roof, clutching his burned throat. When I leap to the next rooftop, he doesn't follow. He'll probably report this to my father. I don't care. My mind is on other things. I have no eyes for the city's splendor tonight. The wind steals the breath from my lungs as I follow my rooftop roadway to what I truly want, and to Sean's apartment.

His windows are dark. There's barely enough room for me to crouch on the windowsill's decorative brickwork, the soles of my boots gripping the brick's rough texture. Sean's asleep, curled on his side with one bare arm draped across the space in his bed where my body should be. He looks smaller, somehow. Lonely. I wonder if he's more upset than he let on, that I've kept my distance.

I should leave before I give in to temptation. I want him. I need him. A few strands of hair rest against his parted lips, begging me to brush them away and kiss him. I rest my hand on the windowpane, but make myself pull away. It's time to go.

As I draw back, my foot slips. I brace against the frame. My knee slams against the glass, rattling it. Sean bolts upright in bed, clutching the sheet to his chest. There's nowhere for me to go but down—but before I can drop over the edge, he squints at me.

"...Tobias?"

I've been caught. I should go—just disappear. But one moment's hesitation and indecision are all he needs to slip out of bed and pad to the window, yawning drowsily. His loose pajama pants hang dangerously low, beneath the hard ridge of his iliac crest. Reaching up, he unbolts the window and lifts the pane, opening a large enough space for me to slip through.

"What are you doing out there?"

I drop into the room and land lightly, sinking into a crouch. As I straighten, I shake my head. "Don't. Don't ask." Grasping his hips, I pull him close. "Don't say anything. Just… be with me."

"Tobias." His eyes soften, and his fingers skim down my cheek.

"Shh." Rising up on my toes, I kiss him. His mouth slants against mine, a perfect fit. Heat rolls through me in an electric surge, and I push him back toward the bed. I need to be in control tonight. I need to have my fill of him, so I never forget. I may be an aberrant—but he makes me human, and that's something I never want to lose.

He lies back on the bed and I strip his clothing away, stroking my hands down his legs. He's beautiful, so beautiful, and I can't resist kissing his shoulders, his chest, teasing little breathy sounds from him with every touch of my lips and hands. The taut pull and flex of his body moves beneath my palms like steel and silk, luring me down until my mouth and tongue trail a searing path over his stomach. When I taste him, he arches, crying out. The scent of him is wild, needful. His cock parts my lips, stretches my mouth, pulses on my tongue with every taste. And when he comes for me, the salt of his flesh lingers on my lips.

He draws me up to kiss me. That taste mingles between us—and as his body meets mine, he fills me until I forget everything but the slow, fluid rhythm between us and the feel of his name on my lips. I hold him as close as I can. He brands every sensation into my memory, until the flash-fire moment comes and washes my mind clean of everything but that trembling pleasure.

When it's over, Sean sinks down against me, his body limp and slick. His brow rests to mine. The tips of our noses touch. "Jesus, Tobias," he gasps, voice soft with wonder.

I can't say anything. I can't do anything but close my eyes and kiss him again, savoring it. I know what this ache is now, this thing that isn't quite pain. Soon I'll smother that bright spark until it's snuffed out, leaving me emptier than ever—but for now it burns hot, consuming. I stroke my fingers over his shoulders, his neck, his chest. I want to tell him I'm sorry, but I can't.

I want to tell him I'm in love with him.

It's not possible. It's not logical. Aberrants cannot love, and the words stick in my throat. I can taste them when our lips part. He sighs and rests his head on my chest. I hate that I have to ruin this.

"I can't stay," I whisper.

"I know."

"How?"

"I just do." He smiles, and I remember that sadness I saw the first night. It's there again, stark and clear, yet still—still, he smiles. "I won't make it difficult for you. Don't worry."

I almost wish he'd get angry. I wish he'd give me a reason to tell him the truth, so at least he'd understand. "It's not like that." I try to sound casual, but my voice is breaking. "I have an early flight. Need to finish packing."

"Mm." Sean looks at me with hooded eyes. "Visiting family for the holidays?"

"Yeah. You?"

He shakes his head. "Too much work. Thought I'd stay here."

"You should go." I tighten my grip. "Back to Clovelly, I mean. See your family. It's Christmas. Work can wait."

He laughs. "Right now? Tobias, that's just daft. A last-minute ticket to England would be staggering."

"I'll pay for it."

"What?" His eyes widen.

I smile weakly. "I'll pay for it. Might as well use my father's money for something that matters." I don't want him in the States when it happens. I don't want him in danger. It will come for him, eventually—but I can at least spare him this.

He stares at me with an odd smile. "You're not making any sense."

"I know. I know, I know, I just—" With a sigh, I make myself relax. "Never mind. I'm being stupid. Kiss me before I go."

I try to make the kiss last as long as possible. Every second is another in which I don't have to let go. Finally, I draw back. Sean ducks his head but can't hide his damp eyes. He knows, somehow, and he doesn't look at me as I rise and dress.

"I'll see you later." He offers a wistful smile.

"Sure," I say, and let myself out.

I'll never see him again.

Chapter Thirteen

My flight doesn't land in D.C. until late evening. Jeremy hasn't spoken a word since he picked me up and drove me to the airport. I can see the bandages beneath his tie and the high neck of his shirt. Throughout the flight, Alice was lost in her own world, listening to the earbuds concealed beneath her shock of red hair. We didn't sit together, and now we lose each other in the crowd as we retrieve our bags and pick up rental cars. My last glimpse of Jeremy is in the Budget parking lot, getting into a green Prius.

We won't be seen together until the day comes. No coordinated activity. No patterns that could alert national security. We don't want them to be prepared. A long, drawn-out battle would undermine my father's precious *statement*.

I check in to my hotel room, a sterile cubicle with wallpaper that looks like an octogenarian's upholstery. We have three days to prepare—no more, no less. Jeremy can't be away from Xinth for more than a few weeks, or the barrier begins to break down and lose cohesion. Travel, backup plans, and the days he spent playing Posable Stalker Batman on my roof haven't left much leeway. Three days to wander D.C., take in the lay of the city, and refine our plan of attack. I'm restless, ready to be done with this, but I have to play holiday tourist. No suspicious movements. I lie in my bed and stare at the ceiling without sleeping. I can't let myself think. If I think, I won't be able to do this.

I don't feel like myself. I don't know who I am anymore, or if I have the strength to put a stop to this.

Or why I even want to.

I'm up with the dawn, snapping pictures of sunrise over the city skyline with a disposable Kodak bought in the hotel gift shop. The passport, ID, and debit card in my pocket say my name is Hirosuke Miyamoto, a salaryman from Narita, in the Chiba prefecture of Japan. I don't speak a word of Japanese. I don't even *look* Japanese—though to some, everyone with dark hair and slanted eyes looks alike.

No one even thinks to question my authenticity when I buy tickets for tours of the White House, the Capitol building, and the Washington Monument. I snap pictures everywhere, blending into the crowd and gazing about with the appropriate wide-eyed wonder.

I just wish it wasn't so damned cold.

In truth, I'm running on autopilot. Spark has taken over and is entirely focused on assessing security in the Capitol building: where the cameras and metal detectors are, where personnel are stationed inside, how the alarm systems are arranged, what areas are accessible to tourists. We plan to infiltrate the building the night before and conceal ourselves inside, long before the House and Senate members arrive. If I'm being honest, I wish we could wait another day or two. The weather forecast promises severe thunderstorms. Tapping into a storm, for me, is like plugging a guitar into an amp. The power inside me escalates from a single steady thrum into a reverberating, soul-trembling wail. But I don't need it. We'll make do without.

As my tour group exits, I glimpse Jeremy in the crowd of new arrivals. I stare blankly past him, pretending to be fascinated by a painting, but catch his quick, seething glance. He's still pouting, then.

Lovely.

Once night falls, I don the guise of Spark and take to the rooftops. In a city like Washington, traveling this way is like flying, using the cables in my gear to rappel down office buildings and swing from high-rise balconies to the sprawling roofs of shopping centers. The lights of D.C. spread out below me, but they aren't my stars, my constellations. It's a cold and alien place, uncaring and dark. Perfect for an aberrant.

I hate it.

In the federal district, Capitol Hill looms majestic, lit against the backdrop of night. The famed Capitol Christmas tree thrusts its spire to the sky as if mimicking the Capitol building's dome, wreathed in lights too bright to see more than the vague shape of a tree. The grounds around the building offer few vantages for aerial surveillance.

I'll have to do this the hard way.

My boots crunch in the snow as I dart through the well-manicured grounds, using the trees for cover. I've never seen snow in person before. Sean told me about it—about winter in Clovelly, and the snow draping over slope-shouldered cottages. He made it sound quaint and magical. This sodden slush is just icy and miserable, soaking the cuffs of my jeans.

After finding a secluded spot in the brush, I crouch and settle in for a long watch. From here I can see the entrance and watch the guards on their rounds. Tomorrow night I'll find a different vantage. Already, I think we'll have to scrap the nighttime infiltration plan and slip in during the day. There's just not enough time for me to learn the security system well enough to short it from the outside without setting it off. We can't do anything that will prevent Congress from convening. One security incident, and they'll cancel the entire assembly to protect their precious politicians.

Faint squeak of footsteps on snow. I whirl, one hand falling to the dagger strapped to my thigh, the other gripping the weighted end of a spool of flexible, conductive wire coiled in my sleeve. A figure stands silhouetted beneath the shadow of a tree's low-hanging branches.

"Spark."

I relax and release my weapons. "Phase," I respond with a nod.

Jeremy steps out into the light, costumed and masked, his identity hidden beneath the persona of Phase. He's visible only a moment before he joins me in my concealment, sinking down to crouch at my side.

"Looks like we had the same idea," he says.

"Where's Torrent?" Alice. Her power lets her control any liquid, even spontaneously generating limited floods condensed from moisture in the air. She and I work well together. Water conducts electricity. A few inches of water on the floor of a room, and everyone with their feet touching the ground dies the moment the current jumps.

"Digging up information on the sprinkler system." Jeremy glances at me from the corner of his eye. "Are you ready for this?"

"Of course."

"Is that so? You've been out of commission for quite a while." The polite lilt to his voice never changes, but the mocking undertone is unmistakable. "Playing human for so long you're even sleeping with one of them. I'm starting to wonder whose side you're on."

"Was I supposed to be a eunuch? I had to blend in.

Humans have friends. Lovers. Are you jealous over a fling?"

"A fling?" He gives a derisive snort. "You're in love with him."

"Love. From an aberrant. Are you out of your mind?"

"You're half-human."

"We're all half-human, you idiot." *No*, I want to say. *Sean is right. We're all human.* "Both your parents were fully human."

"But I'm not, and I never forget that." With a cold look, Jeremy stands. "You'd do well to remember the same. Your status as the Lord High General's son will only protect you so far. Be ready. Do this right. Remember what you are, or my next assignment may be to dispose of his disappointment of a son…young Master."

He melts away into the dark, leaving only his threat to fill the space where he'd stood. In the old days, I would have followed him and shown him his place with brutal certainty. Now, I don't have the heart for it. I hate him for being right. I have to prove myself, come Christmas Eve, or my father will make an example of me.

But first he'll execute Sean before my eyes, as the one responsible for my fall.

Kill over five hundred people, all to save one. Plunge the world into war, just to buy him a little more time. I can't do it. I won't do it.

I have no choice.

Near dawn, I return to the hotel room to eat and catch a few hours of sleep. The food is tasteless, my sleep restless, the pillow a hard lump beneath my head. I am not human, I remind myself. No more than a transgenic mouse is human. So we share genetics. That doesn't matter. Ninety-nine percent of the creatures on the planet share 90 percent of the same genes, give or take. It means nothing. Humans wipe out mice and rats when they become a nuisance. I'm just doing the same on a larger scale, before they can exterminate me.

They're only rats, filthy and weak.

Even Sean.

The next day and night are much the same. Another stakeout, first as Hirosuke, then as Spark. Alice slips blueprints under my hotel room door and spirits away unseen. Jeremy leaves numbers traced into the frost on my window, a ghost making his presence known. By day three, we're ready.

The following morning, I'm the first one in. My gear is in my backpack. One brush against the metal detector, and its signal scrambles. I pass through without incident. A dime-sized piece of chalk in my palm leaves a minuscule yellow mark on the very edge of the detector's frame, unnoticeable unless you're looking for it. Alice and Jeremy will be.

I follow the tour group through the visitor center, then excuse myself to the bathroom. Federal law prohibits security cameras in bathrooms, so there's no one to watch me duck into a stall to change and strap my gear under my coat. Once I've stuffed the empty backpack and my civilian clothes into the toilet tank, I wait until I'm sure the other stalls are empty, then stand on the toilet to pry the panel from the air vent. I have to work quickly, before anyone walks in.

It only takes a moment to yank the panel free, haul myself into the ventilation duct, then slide the panel back into place. The blueprints, retrieved from my back pocket, guide me through the network of ducts. It's cramped and smells musty, but I manage to squeeze through until I find my appointed position. Through a vent cover, I look down on the floor of the House Chamber, with its tiered seats and dark, wood-paneled walls. It's a waiting game now. I find a comfortable position and close my eyes against the bars of light falling through the slats. I don't like the silence, the stillness. It's too easy to drift into thought, and from there…memory.

Sean's laughter. The rough, sure grip of his hands; the heat of his caress. His eyes flashing when he challenges everything

I believe, everything I stand for.

Maybe he's been right all this time.

Alice joins me not long before the lights below wink out for the night. The stylized silver swirls on her formfitting blue latex bodysuit catch the lingering remnants of illumination. She offers me a brief, tense smile, electric with anticipation. She's nearly quivering.

"This is it," she whispers. "It's finally our time."

I avoid her eyes. "Phase?"

"Already in position."

"Then we wait."

She settles at my side. Her earbuds are back. She falls silent, and I close my eyes again. With Alice here, it's easier to close myself off. I can't show emotion in front of her; she'd see it as weakness. My father always says one can never show weakness to a subordinate, or an enemy. They'll eat you alive.

I wonder if that was his rationale for killing my mother, or if he even needed a reason. She was human, after all. Disposable. All he needed from her was an heir.

The night passes without incident. Occasionally I hear Alice moving, the crinkle of cellophane as she eats something, and for a few minutes her warmth disappears from my side when she mutters something about the bathroom. I don't open my eyes until well into morning. The doors below open, and the clamor of voices reaches up to warn me.

It's time.

I stretch from my cramped position and shift to my knees. The senators and representatives are a cloud of dark suits and stiff hair, milling about below. It's easy to pick out the reporters by their microphones and more relaxed clothing. Uniformed security personnel flank every door, firearms on their hips. They'll have to go first. We may be superhuman, but we aren't immune to bullets.

One of the reporters catches my attention. He walks

hunched over, trailing close to another chattering group. A long coat shrouds his body; a wide-brimmed hat hides his face. I frown. Strange, but there's no time to worry about it now. Probably Secret Service, trying to play at being undercover and failing, that body language problem all over again, giving him away. It doesn't matter.

He'll die with the others.

I check my watch. Twenty-two minutes. The numbers on my window were times. The session will convene in seventeen minutes. Five minutes after the doors close, we'll move. My father is probably in the building somewhere. Now that I think about it, he could even be that reporter. He'll make his appearance when the time is right.

I shift into a crouch and, pulling my gloves off, nudge Alice's arm. She opens her eyes and puts her earbuds away. I flash two fingers, then two again, and she nods. The minutes count down. With each one I feel a little colder, a little more hollow. If I don't do this, thousands of aberrants will die, and millions of others may never have the chance to be born. A few thousand aberrants have more value than a hundred million humans. *They* are my people. Not humans. I close my eyes and repeat it until I believe it. It must be done. It *must* be done.

It's time. The congressmen and congresswomen settle in their seats. The doors close with an echoing *clang*. The armed officers take their positions before the exits. Whispering noise fills the room as people shuffle through their papers, leaning over to murmur to each other. The Speaker of the House moves to the tiered dais. His voice fills the suddenly quiet room.

"I now call this joint session of Congress—"

Alice presses her hand to the wall of the ventilation duct. The sprinklers dotting the ceiling of the House Chamber spin and spurt. Jets of water spray over the room, soaking everyone in seconds. Shrieks and shouts rise, confused calls, panicked questions: *Is there a fire? Where's the fire? Should we evacuate?*

"Everybody to the exits!" one of the guards shouts. That's my cue. I kick out the ventilation grate and drop through, plummeting to the dais. My boots strike the hollow desk hard enough to raise a deafening boom. Binders and stacks of sodden paper scatter around me.

Every eye turns to me as I stand from my crouch. I can feel the guards' weapons trained on me, their deadly intent like a touch scraping my skin. The sprinklers sheet over me like the rain of the monsoon, cold and clinging wet.

"Sorry to interrupt." The massive chamber picks up my voice and carries it in spreading echoes. I don't even recognize myself. Spark's voice is authoritarian, cold, confident, with a malicious edge. It's like listening to someone else move my lips. "I have a few items to add to today's agenda."

A squat, balding senator barks, "Just what do you think you're doing? Is this a terrorist attack?" He looks ridiculous, cringing away from the water with his suit coat pulled over his head.

"I'm here on behalf of the nation of Xinth." Indrawn breaths and shrill screams surround me. There's a part of me that still enjoys this—that moment of recognition, the fear, the chaos just before they die. "You may have heard of me. My name is Spark. I speak and act for the Lord High General Infernus Blaze." I smile. "We'd like to have a word with you."

A moment of stunned stillness, and panic takes over. Before the guards can fire their weapons, a crush of surging bodies forces them against the doors—but the doors won't open. Jeremy had come through right on time, liquefying the doors, the hinges, and the frames long enough to fuse them into one piece, then solidifying them again into an unbreakable wall. The members of Congress are trapped, and it only takes them a few moments to realize it. Palpable ripples of terror flow through the crowds. While I watch the hysteria, Alice drops down to take her place at my side.

I raise my voice. "If you'll all take your seats again, please."

They barely notice, screaming and trampling each other to get to doors that won't budge. I signal Alice with a nod. She smirks and tilts her head toward one of the security guards. He lets out a strangled noise that turns into a horrific, inhuman shriek. His skin swells and bubbles. Within seconds he bursts apart, showering the nearby congressmen and the massive double doors with a wet crimson pulp that used to be a man. They skitter away, faces blank with fear, right before a second guard explodes. It's a trick of Alice's I've always been fond of: forcing the blood inside the human body to expand, tearing it apart from the inside out.

Odd how it's not as entertaining as it used to be.

Jeremy steps through the wall, the wood paneling briefly dissolving, reforming once he's passed. The two guards stationed nearby whirl, drawing and taking aim, but the metal of their guns drips through their fingers in a slick ooze. Jeremy shrugs with an innocent smile.

"Let's try this again," I say. This time, silence falls. Fear is a wonderful motivator. "As I said, return to your seats. Quietly, please." I raise my hand. Arcs of sizzling blue-white leap between my fingers. "In case anyone gets any ideas, I'd like to remind you that water is an excellent conductor of electricity, and all of you are quite terribly wet."

Their murmurs are subdued and rebellious, but they obey. They always obey. Sheep running from the dogs nipping at their heels. That's all they are, I tell myself. All they are. I can do this.

"Wh-what do you want?" a woman asks, her voice quavering. The nameplate says she's Ruby Martinez, Iowa. My smile widens.

"Ask your colleague Senator Cranston. He's brought you here to vote on mass murder. The genocide of an entire race."

Every head turns toward Cranston. The man sits stiff in his chair, white beneath his tan, but he's still defiant. The cameras are rolling. He has to put on a good face.

"What do you want?" Scorn drips from his every word. The scorn of the righteous, so very certain of his cause. "You want me to tear up the bill? Because I won't. You people are sick. You're dangerous. Curing you is an act of mercy. If we can save people from becoming like you, I'll—"

"Spark," Alice lisps in a high sing-song voice. "He talks too much. Should I shut him up?"

"Not yet." I tilt my head slowly. "I want him to watch this. I want him to know he's responsible for this. We have our own proposal, and we've already voted: you all die."

"I might have a few objections to that."

A strong voice cuts over the frightened, indignant clamor. On the upper tier, the man in the hat and coat rises, and I realize in all the panic he never moved, never even left his seat. Now, as he stands, both hat and coat fall away to reveal a clinging bodysuit in fitted black rubber, grooved and segmented but otherwise patterned only by the sculpture of his body. As he steps around the railing a wind ripples through the room, creating a crosscurrent of silver waves across the falling spray. When he drops over the edge the wind wraps around him in a spiraling embrace, and he drifts gracefully to the central floor.

Recognition weighs cold in my gut. The mask hides half his face, but I know that voice. I know the long black hair slicking to his neck, shoulders, back. I've watched those pale eyes darken with passion, kissed those lips, left bruising bite marks on that jaw, explored every inch of the body displayed so sinfully by the suit.

The blood drains from my face, leaving me dizzy. My hand falls and I can only stare, barely managing a croaking whisper.

"...Sean?"

Chapter Fourteen

It makes perfect sense now, and none at all. The strange questions. The string of failed relationships, never letting them get too close to the truth. The careful way he spoke of running from something; running from his human family so he wouldn't hurt them, wouldn't force them to live with what he is. The aberrant terrorist attack foiled by one of their own, and the windstorm that rescued a couple from armed robbery. The behavioral medication in the cabinet. Even his presence at Langdon's. He was investigating, the same as I. I'm an idiot for not seeing it before.

No. I was a blind, lovesick fool.

And look where it got me. Stupid enough to miss what was right in front of my face, because I didn't want to see it. I didn't even want to consider the possibility, but now I can't deny the truth.

Sean's an aberrant. An aberrant who feels, who cares, who believes in the inherent rightness of things and the inborn goodness of people, who laughs with that mixture of joy and sadness too real to be an act.

He's an aberrant who fights to protect rather than destroy, and I don't know how that's possible.

How is he not as broken and damaged as the rest of us? How can he believe the things he does, when humans would slaughter him if they knew?

I can't take my eyes away from him, and I can't miss the moment his heart breaks. The moment he looks at my face and, despite the mask, knows me for who and what I am: a monster, reflected in his eyes with cold certainty.

"Tobias…?" he whispers, his voice thick. The color flees from his skin to leave his lips white, and he sinks to his knees on the soggy and pooling carpet. "You're—you've—but… Langdon? All…all those *people*…" His chest hitches in a shuddering breath. "How could you? *How?*"

My throat closes. "I told you." My lips tremble, until I clench my jaw. I can't do this. I can't *feel* this, horrid and thick and oozing like poison mud inside my chest. There's no room for it inside me, and it doesn't belong. "We're monsters. You should have listened."

It shouldn't hurt like this. The way he looks at me, the shock in his eyes, the betrayal. I can't move. I can't speak. This is all falling apart, and once again I'm not sure why all these people have to die.

"So the lovers reunite." Jeremy's silken, derisive laughter rings over the room. "Don't tell me this mincing little thing wants to play *hero*."

There's barely a moment's warning, a warping and rippling, before the carpet beneath Sean liquefies into a pool. Without thinking, I throw myself from the dais and slam into him, shoving him aside just as the carpet thrusts upward in a hardening spike. We tumble across the floor together, fetching up against the first tier of seats and sending people skittering back with shrilling cries. I try to shield him with my body, but we both hit with a painful *thud*.

Pushing myself up on my arms, I snarl, "What the hell are you doing here?"

"Me? What about you!" His eyes blaze. "I came to *talk* to them. To show them there are real people affected by this law. To convince them there's another way. Not to *kill* them."

It's almost enough to make me laugh. Spark's laughter, cold and mocking, for the naïveté of it. Sean's on the wrong side of this fight. But I can't laugh when I—the real me, the man under the mask—am torn apart inside, and I want to tell him to get out, run, get as far away from here as possible before I have to do something to him more terrible than any punishment a human can inflict.

But before I can speak, the table behind him liquefies to sludge and splashes down in a heavy wave. I grab his arm and pull him out of the way; he flings a hand out. A wall of wind whips in front of us, sheeting water aside. The fluid wood pulp splashes against the swirling tempest, sprays everywhere, recedes like the tide.

Whirling on me, Sean shoves me. "Let go!" He rips his arm from my grip. "I knew you were lying about something, but not something like *this*. I slept with you. I *slept* with a mass murderer, a—a—a dictator's bloody lapdog!" He thrusts back from me, his eyes burning with accusation. "I loved you!"

He loved me. *Loved*. Past tense. That stings more than being called what I am: a lapdog. I don't know if my heart is soaring or crumbling to pieces. I don't have time to wonder.

"So now we know which side you're on, Spark." Jeremy saunters closer, Alice drifting behind him like a shadow. The sprinkler's shower doesn't touch her, eddying away to swirl around her shoulders in liquid ribbons. He smirks. "Are you ready to die for these humans, then?"

I push myself to one knee, keeping my body between Sean and Jeremy, but when I search for words I find none. Because I'm not ready to die for these humans. Never for *them*.

But for Sean?

I think I would.

And that terrifies me, fear starker than any I can remember feeling since the night I woke to the chilling sound of my mother's scream, counterpoint to the low, calm certainty of my father's voice, soothing her into the black.

I'm not doing this. I *can't*. The choke chain around my neck is tighter than ever, but it's real. Whatever this thing was with Sean wasn't. I can't *feel* love. This is just an echo of longing, a game of pretend that I've told myself is real because I want to feel *something*. Something true, something honest, something as deep as the passion with which humans live their mayfly lives. It was just a fantasy.

And now it's over.

I have a choice to make. The decision cuts deep, and I tell myself it doesn't hurt, doesn't feel like a mortal wound to my heart even when I know that's a blatant lie. But it's what I have to do, or Jeremy and Alice will kill us both.

In the seconds that have passed while I fought through the morass of my thoughts, Jeremy and Sean have locked on each other, staring, tense and silent. I steel myself and look over my shoulder at Sean. My hand flattens against the soaked carpet, cold and bristly against my palm.

"You'll want to make your exit now." I can't believe the smooth, cutting lilt of my own voice. It's ugly. Nasty-sweet. Almost enticing. The puppet master Spark is moving my lips again, making me sound far too much like my father. "The second the current jumps, everyone here dies. You might survive, but you'll be a wanted man. No one will believe you weren't part of this. Especially when I make sure your name and face are plastered on every news channel between here and the UK. You'll never have a normal life again, and you'll have nowhere to run. Unless you run now."

Behind his mask, Sean's eyes widen briefly. A flash of

hurt. A flash of horror. Before they close over, glassy mirrors locking away anything he might feel for me, anything I might be able to carve out of him. He, too, has another self. A secret self. And with the words I've spoken, I've lost all access to him. To the beautiful man who held me down and gave me his love in breathless sighs and the painfully wonderful rhythm of flesh to flesh. The aberrant was never the secret inside his heart.

It was the truth of who he was, and the love he gave to me.

That love is absent from his voice when he speaks, replaced by condemnation, contempt in every precisely stated word. "You want me to run to save myself. When you'll kill these people anyway, whether I'm here or not."

Several congressmen mutter and there's a shrill scream, but they're too frightened to move; I can smell it on them, filling the room with a sour yellow stink.

I curl my upper lip. The sparks are already building inside me, waiting to rise to my skin, waiting to connect and sizzle across the puddles pooling on the carpet. I should do it. *Do it*, instead of trying to reason with him like I think I can somehow save him. From the humans. From himself.

From me.

"You're outnumbered," I spit. "Or do you think they'll fight for their lives? They're *weak*. Cowardly. They'll let you die for them, and spit on your corpse for it. Or do you expect them to *thank* you?"

I don't expect his smile. Tired. Sad. I'm the one who put that smile on his lips. "I don't need them to thank me. I don't need anything, but you can't understand that, can you? I'm not like you, *Spark*. Human lives are worth just as much as mine. I'm only sorry I couldn't make you understand that." His lips tighten. His eyes close. "And I'm sorry that I have to hurt you."

Hearing that name from his lips tears me to pieces,

freezes me in place. That moment of shock, of pain, is all it takes to catch me off guard. He raises a clenched fist, thrusts it out, and a shock of air slams into me like a wrecking ball, knocking me back with a hot, dull burst of pain in the center of my chest, breaking my contact with the floor and whipping me into the air before I can manage more than a single static shock—blue-white arcs that fly from my fingers and dissipate in midair. Alice's and Jeremy's cries seem distant as I tumble high, tossed end over end like I'm in a goddamned dryer, my heart and my stomach swapping places over and over again, the others just scraps of color flashing past as the room whips by in a spinning cyclone worse than a fucking Tilt-a-Whirl on PCP.

I'm going to throw up. Or pass out. I can't afford to do either. I've got a split second to react, a split second to save myself, because when he drops me it's going to *hurt*. There—a lantern fixture, jutting out from the upper edge of the wall. I've got to time this just right. I've got to *focus*. I can't afford to look, to see what the massive *crash* I hear is, why people are screaming, why the lights are flickering, when I'm waiting for the next time the twister spins me back. My coat snaps around me, smacks me in the face, blinds me, and in the back of my mind I curse my fucking father and his fucking costumes before it comes: that moment. That moment when I've got a clear shot. The weighted end of the spool of wire on my wrist drops into my hand. I snap it out as hard as I can, gauging against the force of the wind. The wire goes shooting out, sailing across the room, and then it's gone as I'm spun around again. I can't see if it hits the mark or not, but for four-five-*six* milliseconds I'm calling on every bodhisattva I can until something suddenly jerks me back, yanking my arm out to its full length and nearly ripping my shoulder from its socket.

Thank the *narakas*, the weight caught. The wire is wrapped around the neck of the light fixture, barely anchored in place by the flared metal hood, and I'm dangling at the end like a fish on a hook, swinging back and forth on the end of my tether. I force back vertigo, grip the wire in both hands, and pull myself swiftly, hand over hand, against the buffeting wind. In seconds I've swung myself to the wall and braced my feet in a crouch, hanging from the wire like I'm playing Spider-Man. Catching my breath, I take a moment to reorient myself and figure out what the *fuck* is going on while my head's still spinning and every inch of my body is on fire with pain.

The room is a wreck. What's left of it anyway. Sean's blown the fused doors right out of the frames and reduced an entire wall to nothing but studs and sticks of rebar surrounded by the rubble of wood paneling and sheetrock and concrete, with cables hanging and sparking over the empty space spilling out into the hall. A few of the politicians are scrambling over the rubble, but the majority are flattened against the wall. Sean hovers over the room like a god of the storm, his hair whipping around him. Jeremy and Alice are caught in their own personal tornadoes, hovering in midair and spinning so fast it's no wonder Alice has passed out—though Jeremy's flailing, and it'll be only moments before he gets his bearings and does something dangerous. Something I should want him to do. I should be helping him. Helping Alice. Bringing Sean down and tearing him to pieces for betraying his own kind.

But I can't move.

I can only watch Sean as he descends to the dais, graceful and completely in control of himself. Of this situation. He's strong. Stronger than I'd ever imagined my sad-eyed, pensive, lovely professor could be, even if I've no right to call him *mine* anymore. He hasn't noticed yet that I've broken free. Or maybe he just doesn't care. Maybe he knows he's strong enough to tear me apart, and I'm nothing to him.

Not anymore.

"*Move*, you fools," he snarls, and a few more politicians

scurry into motion, clambering over their seats and down toward the closest escape. Sean's head snaps up as the sounds of booted feet echo down the hall with the unmistakable metallic clatter of soldiers running with automatic weapons. With a soft curse under his breath, he sweeps his arm out. The frozen politicians scream as hard gusts of air wrap around them, lift them off their feet, and spill them toward the destroyed wall like tossed dice. I realize Sean's not afraid of the soldiers.

He's just trying to get the humans away from *us* before this clusterfuck reaches epic and bloody proportions.

The moment the humans find their feet, they run, shrieking and tripping over each other, nearly fighting each other to escape in a wild stampede. Sean lifts his head, looking up at me. For just a moment, our eyes meet. His are hard, ferocious, alight with an almost terrifying fire. I feel as if my soul has been plucked from my chest, weighed, found lacking, and left to crumble to dust in his hand.

Then he turns, vaulting down from the dais and taking off at a run, slipping toward one of the back doors. I lose him in the crowd of humans. I should chase him. Stop him. Exact revenge for what he's done to our plan, to Jeremy, to Alice, to me, even if nothing he's done to us could match the depth of what I've done to him by crushing him yet again and carving that lonely weariness inside him just a little bit deeper.

Maybe that's what keeps me in place. Maybe that's why I remain dangling from the wire, doing nothing, saying nothing, only watching him until I can't see even a glimpse of his hair, his costume. The wind filling the room abruptly stops. Jeremy and Alice fall to the floor, plummeting to strike with fleshy, awful *thuds* and lying there in crumpled heaps.

Sean let them go. He's left us alive. More mercy than we'd ever have given him. I don't know how to feel about that. I don't know how to feel about anything. I can only seem to fixate on one thought.

He's gone.

He's gone, but the soldiers aren't. The Secret Service agents. They pour to fill every point of entry, just a blur of suits and uniforms and light sparking off the angry mouths of rifles, service pistols, dozens of weapons pointed right at me. There's shouting, something about dropping my weapons and putting my hands up.

I *am* the weapon.

And I drop myself, a flick of my wrist unspooling the wire suspending me from the light fixture. Bullets spray in my wake as I fall and hit the floor hard, crashing into debris before rolling behind a thick paneled desk. Puffs of sawdust explode over the top of the desk as bullets zing into it, nearly punching through. A few more hits and it'll crumble. I can't risk frying the soldiers, not when Jeremy and Alice are helpless, unconscious. What was once our advantage has become our trap. I might be able to arc a charge across the soaked floor to take out the first line of soldiers, but Jeremy and Alice would get caught in the current.

I shouldn't care. I shouldn't care about *anything*. Self-preservation above all, emotionless and cold, and the only thing that should matter to me is that Jeremy is necessary to maintain the barrier around Xinth, and if the humans capture him or Alice alive, they may be tortured into revealing critical information. But Sean must have me more fucked up than I realized, because right now I'm not thinking about practicality.

I'm thinking about the fact that even if both Jeremy and Alice would kill me in a heartbeat if my father ordered it, they're still *my people*...and I can't just leave them here.

I picked a hell of a time to develop a sense of loyalty.

A bullet bursts through the desk in a hail of splinters and embeds in the wall behind me. I fling myself to the side just as the hailstorm of slugs pellets the desk and shreds it into kindling. Just a moment in the open before I'm diving behind the dais, circling the room, ducking low and ignoring the throbbing pain of my bruised, tired body. It's the most fucked up game of tag ever, gunfire chasing me as I duck and dive through the scattered rubble to a massive chunk of concrete from the shattered wall, tumbled right next to the opening where soldiers line up like they're taking turns at a shooting gallery.

Crimson bursts through me in a gut-wrenching shot of pain as I fling myself behind the concrete slab. I collapse against it, gasping for breath, and reach down to touch the rip in my jeans, just over my outer thigh. A trench parts the flesh beneath, a bullet graze that burns like acid poured into the raw wound, blood mingling with the water soaking the black denim. I can't see how deep it is when it's pumping so profusely, but blood flow that fast probably means they nicked an artery—and if I don't get this stitched up soon, I'll be passing out in short order.

This is really starting to piss me off.

I've got one shot. The entire reason I risked that little obstacle course. I tilt my head back. Over the top of the concrete slab, those sparking electrical wires still twist and lash. I can use them. Tap into the current to amplify my own power, and use the wires to direct the burst away from the room's interior so I don't fry my companions. I'll only be exposed for a second. That should be enough. Granted, it's also enough to get shot, and I have no idea why the hell I'm doing this when letting Jeremy be captured or killed will save me from having to account for myself when he reports back to my father.

No. I know why.

Because Sean would want me to, and I can't forget that look of condemnation in his eyes.

I close my eyes with a curse, then push myself up. Moralizing can wait until later. I risk a glance around the edge of the concrete slab, and immediately jerk back when a bullet chips off a chunk of cement where my head had been. They're going to get sick of shooting uselessly at concrete pretty soon, and either swarm the room or start shooting at Jeremy and Alice to make sure they stay down. Standing hurts, but I move quickly—shrugging out of my coat, flattening my back against the slab, bracing myself to jump.

It's a one-two count: throw my coat out to the side in a distracting flutter of black, and twist to leap up to the top of the slab, grip the edge, and pull myself up. I can't pause, can't think, can't do anything but *move*. Bullets slash my coat to pieces. I have half a second to coil myself into a crouch at the top of the shorn-off edge of cement, brace my feet, then *leap*, stretching my body out as long as I can to *reach*. My hand snaps around a jutting strut of rebar, bracing me enough to pull myself up and catch at one of the sparking cables. Don't blink. Don't flinch. Don't think about the lives I'm about to take to save my own. Those thoughts are a corruption inside me, and they'll kill me.

The moment I come into contact with the copper wiring bristling from the shredded end of the cable, I come alight. I'm a lightning rod, a conduit, and the electricity that flows into me feels as if it fills the void where my heart should be. Where Sean should be, pouring into my veins in a white-hot rush, the other half of myself that I need to be whole. When I was a boy, when I first learned that I had these powers, I'd play with electrical sockets. Climb poles and toy with the power lines. Feed off the electricity like a parasite, because it felt like a living thing that made me feel more alive than anything in my empty life.

And it fills me now: a rush, the pouring explosion of a lover spilling inside my body, deep and fulfilling and penetrating, trembling through every inch of me. I come ablaze. I can feel the entire D.C. grid connected through these simple lines, waiting for me to tap into it, power ready to overflow the boundaries of my flesh, making me a god. It's addictive. It's destructive. I could tear this entire building apart.

But I don't.

I can barely see past the blinding white crackles around me. But in the second it's taken me to charge, the vague shapes of the soldiers have turned toward me, their shouts struggling not to be screams, their breaths almost louder than the sizzle and pop. All it takes is one twist of will. One voluntary muscle reflex, as easy as flexing my arm. Power floods from me in a directed blast: a wave of sizzling lashes, writhing and crawling, pouring over the soldiers and Secret Service agents and lashing them with lightning whips, jumping like chain lightning from body to body without ever touching the ground. For a moment everything is white.

Then it fades, and they're nothing but a smoking heap of bodies on the floor, their guns half-fused into useless messes.

But they're breathing.

I might have shocked one or two hearts into stopping. But there'll be EMTs in here in no time, defibrillators, and no Spark to fuck them up and stop them from working this time. I've never done this before. Controlled my power enough to let them *live*. I don't know how to feel about it. I don't know how to feel at *all*, except drained after bleeding out so much current, like it took a piece of me with it.

But there'll be more humans arriving by the second. Time to move. This mission is done, over. My father's coup has failed on national television. I let go of the rebar and drop, landing hard—then buckling when my injured thigh goes weak beneath me. Hissing, I clutch at it, trying to staunch the bleeding, to dull the livid pulse of pain as I stagger upright and limp toward Jeremy and Alice. There's no time to be gentle. I can't carry them both alone. I slap Jeremy across the face hard enough to make my palm sting. He moans, his lashes fluttering, but he doesn't wake until I shock him with a quick, carefully controlled sizzle.

His breaths suck in. He jolts upright, sitting up like Frankenstein's monster come to life, his eyes snapping open and his hand clutching his chest. "Wh-what the f—"

"On your feet." I offer him my hand. "Help me with Alice. We've got five minutes to get out of here, or we're not getting out at all."

Jeremy looks up at me, his blank eyes clearing. What I see when the clouds part isn't promising. There's recrimination. Accusation. Disgust. But worse—satisfaction, as if I've played right into his hands. Maybe I have. Maybe he recognized this quiet, confused ache, this longing to be human, long before I ever knew it was burning inside me. For a moment the corners of his lips twitch, before setting grimly as he takes my hand and pulls himself up. He doesn't say a word. His obedience is implicit in his silence, in the way he dutifully—almost too dutifully—bends to help me sling Alice's arms over our shoulders.

But this isn't over.

And every word he doesn't say tells me I've made a fatal mistake.

Chapter Fifteen

There's something far more disturbing about Jeremy's capacity to heal than his capacity to destroy.

Or maybe I only feel that way because it's my flesh he's molding like putty, and I'd rather watch a thousand people liquefied into a sludge of meat and bone soup than watch my own thigh muscle squelching and shifting around while the skin stretches over it in a rubbery sheet. I sit on the bed in my hotel room, staring at the wall, focusing on the pain in my thigh rather than the thousand other things I can't bear to think about right now, can't even *process*. All I can see when I close my eyes is green eyes rimmed by a black mask. Alice is stretched along the bed at my back, still unconscious, while Jeremy kneels before me — bruised, but whole.

I make myself watch him work from the corner of my eye, but I won't lie: I'm about to throw up. I don't consider myself squeamish — I can't be, working in an animal testing lab and slaughtering local citizenry on behalf of my despotic father — but that?

That's just *nasty*.

Nasty, but necessary. It's a temporary stopgap; he's done it before, fusing wounds closed to keep me and others from bleeding out. It doesn't heal the cells; just forms a flesh patch to keep the blood inside my body and dull the nerve endings. He's done the same to staunch Alice's internal bleeding. Later, when we're safe, we'll need real medical attention. I'll likely need stitches. Alice will need the intensive care unit. She's out for the count. Whatever plans we make can't include her.

Plans. Like there's any plan other than getting the hell out of here—if we even can, when the nation's capital is on lockdown and high alert. The TV's on, the news filling the tense silence with its high-energy blatt, spouting a sensationalized recap of our exploits with that mixed combination of panic and the sort of lewd, voyeuristic glee that keeps people tuning in even when they're terrified and tired. My face is all over every channel, glowing translucent and strange with the surge pouring through me—exactly what I'd threatened Sean with. But in the end, I have the safe borders of Xinth to protect me.

Sean doesn't, even if my father's fear tactics will probably eventually drive him and every other aberrant to Xinth as a last resort.

One way or another. Anything to feel safe in a world that hates us. It's a feeling I understand far too well.

I'd kill to feel safe right now. We barely made it away in the chaos of soldiers, helicopters, even a row of mobilized tanks. Only one critical moment to vanish into the trees on the Capitol building grounds before anyone caught sight of us, cursing that open space that had once been an inconvenience and was now a life-threatening obstacle. We'd hid in the branches for nearly half an hour while they combed the building for us, until we found our moment to slip away, ascend to the rooftops, and limp our way back to climb in through the window of the hotel. I can't help but laugh, short and choked, thinking of the three of us coming in through the front door, limping and bloody in our tattered costumes, with Alice dragged between me and Jeremy. I don't think the humans would've even known what to do.

Jeremy flicks a hard look up at me. "You think this is funny?" He pulls his hand from my thigh and stands, a snarl stretching his lips. "What the *fuck* was that?"

Before I can overthink it, I backhand him as hard as I can, clenched fist smashing across his face—surging to my feet and putting my entire body into it until the meaty *smack* of impact reverberates up my sore arm into my wrenched shoulder. I don't have a choice. We're pack animals, under my father's rule. And if I don't remind him of his place in the pack order, he'll try to usurp mine.

He drops like his legs have been cut from beneath him, a red blot already starting to bloom on his cheek and jaw. Gasping, he lies there, his eyes wide and stunned as he gingerly touches his face with fingers still stained with my blood.

"Don't," I bite off coldly. "Don't ever speak to me that way. Remember who you serve."

Just a week ago, he would have bowed his head in submission, his expression carefully masked and neutral, and said, *Yes, young Master. Of course, young Master,* before slinking away. But now he looks up at me with a sneer, his brows twisted together into angry ridges, and part of me wants so spitefully to ask him how he fucking *feels* because right now he's sure as hell not the emotionless, perfect automaton we're supposed to be.

"You don't get to play the princeling now, *young Master*. Not when you're hardly worthy of the title."

He smirks, starting to sit up—until I slam the sole of my boot against his throat and shove him back down to the carpet, thudding his head against the floor. "He caught me off guard." I grind my heel slowly, digging the treads into his neck, listening to him gag and choke with every deliberate movement. "You won't. Don't push me."

He arches, gripping at my boot, sucking in wet-sounding breaths, but I hold for another long ten count, not letting him up until I'm good and ready. I lift my foot just enough to let him breathe, let him speak. Waiting. Daring him to talk back to me again. It will be the last time. It's less the disrespect I care about and more getting out of this alive, without waiting for him to stab me in the back the moment I risk blinking. I don't have time for this right now, but if he wants to play power games, it ends now.

Wordless, we stare each other down. The moment something changes inside him, I can see it. As clearly as if the want had written itself on his face in eldritch script, I see it: the urge to use his power against me. To petrify my skin and turn my innards into vapor boiling inside a hardened shell. Only we both know he'd be dead before he could do more than minor damage, the very atoms comprising his cellular makeup flying apart and destabilizing with every electron lost. It's the same effect as massive doses of ionizing radiation, compressed into seconds. He'd be safer locked in the core of a nuclear reactor without protective gear — and he knows it.

He knows, and after long moments his eyes lower. He goes limp, practically showing belly, and turns his face away. I can't trust that he's not faking me out, but I can't hold him there forever. Kill him now, or let him up. Those are my only options.

Even if letting him up just means delaying the problem until later.

Human lives are worth just as much as mine, Sean whispers inside my head, and I grit my teeth.

Leave me alone. You were nothing. You're just another problem to be dealt with.

And yet I step back. I let Jeremy go and leave him to pick himself up off the floor. I know it's foolish of me to turn my back on him, but it sends a message.

You're nothing to me.

My Bluetooth pings in my ear. I glance over my shoulder at Jeremy—sulking Jeremy, slouched in a chair and peeling out of his scarred, ripped latex—then move to the window, brushing the curtains aside briefly to watch several helicopters go racing past, heading toward the Capitol building; above a fighter jet soars, scraping the sky with its hoarse roar. I track the smoke trails, pressing my lips together tightly, then make myself answer, tapping the earpiece.

"Here."

I know it's him before he speaks. My father. That rolling, smooth voice never rises, but there's an edge to it that tells me with one word that he's not pleased.

"Report."

"Aberrant interference. Someone tried to play hero. Someone I think has been playing hero under the radar for a while."

As if those neutral words, the careful absence of names and identities, could mask what really happened. As if he wouldn't know. I know better. He watches everything. All-seeing eyes, making sure nothing deviates from his order. Not his empire. Not his son.

"You let a sexual entanglement make you weak," he says. "You could have prevented this."

"What do you want me to say? Do you expect me to deny it?"

"At least you aren't wasting my time with excuses or apologies."

I say nothing. There's nothing to say. No point. It happened. It's entirely possible I'm going back to Xinth only to be executed. But at the moment there's no reason to talk about it.

After a moment of steely silence, he continues. "It's not a

complete loss. You disrupted Congress and escaped alive. The cameras on the floor caught enough footage of the destruction for viral media traction. A demonstration of power worthy of human fear and paranoia."

I close my eyes and drag my hand down my face. I'm not in the mood for megalomaniac plotting right now. I want to punch something. Or fuck something, but right now both my options hate me, and I wouldn't touch one of those two with someone else's dick. Guess which.

"The kind of fear and paranoia that will lead to even harsher legislation, passed swiftly and unanimously. Not the cowed submission you were aiming for." Back talk isn't doing me any favors right now. I don't care. "There'll be a violent military response. Global. It won't just be the States anymore, because now one failed attack will make them think if they just marshal enough military force, they'll have a chance to win."

His utter lack of response says more than any words. Seconds tick by without a sound. Seconds that sink deeper and deeper into me with a realization so cold my spine becomes a column of ice, my breaths become frost.

"You wanted that," I whisper. "You want to push this into escalating global conflict."

Still he says nothing. I can't bite my tongue on this, play the reasoned objector, hold back and dance carefully around his fury. I *can't*. And I whirl on Jeremy, glaring at him. I can hardly breathe.

"Get out," I bark, and when he just freezes, looking at me blankly, my voice rises, snapping with a rage that sounds nothing like Spark, nothing like Tobias, nothing like anything I know of myself or my alter ego. "*Get out!*"

The look of stunned, almost fearful confusion on his face would be gratifying if I wasn't sick to my core. He remains motionless for a heartbeat longer, then rises quickly, wraps the hotel-issue courtesy bathrobe over his costume, and slips out into the hall. He can stay there for all I care, or slink back to lick his wounds at whatever cheap motel he booked for himself. Once the door closes, I prod Alice hard enough to rock her limp body, but she's well and truly out. Dragging a hand through my hair, I pace the floor, struggling to find the words to say, but it's all chaos. Chaos and frustration and a sense of helpless *wrongness*, and I don't even know where to start.

"Is there something you wish to say to me?" my father asks, and the dam breaks.

"How narcissistic *are* you?" I explode, flinging a hand out in a sharp gesture as if he can see me. "You're doing this just to incite massive global response. You're like a child throwing a tantrum at a party for as much attention as possible. Because single coordinated airstrikes and tactical attempts at infiltration aren't enough for you, are they? You don't just want to subjugate the humans. You want them to *react* to you with the gravity you feel you deserve. Surrender would be boring, when you could have carnage and carve your legacy in scorched earth and blood."

His sigh is weary, almost patronizing. "Do you expect me to explain myself to you?"

"Spark would never expect the *Lord High General* to explain himself. But I'm asking my fucking father to, damn it."

Pointless. He's never been my father. Just a sperm donor. And I don't expect him to answer.

But he does.

"Humans are complacent." Steady words. So hypnotic, so convincing that it's almost too easy to want to accept them, as I always have. "So complacent that even now, we are only someone else's problem. Something for the military to deal with. Even though we could be their neighbors, their friends, their lovers"—that stings, and make no mistake; it's deliberate—"they brush it off for yet another day. I will not be brushed off, Tobias. *We* will not be brushed off. They will look at us face to face. They will feel this come home to roost. It is not the military reaction I desire. It is the awakening of the everyday populace. The awareness of the reality they live in now, and the shock of knowing how tenuous their position truly is."

"…Yeah."

I feel like I'm gumming the word, this dry, tacky thing rolling around my mouth, meaningless and gathering dust. I don't know what else to say, because deep down every word he says makes *sense*. It echoes everything I'd thought before, about human complacency. About the superficial way they care as long as it's just something they can shake their heads over while it always affects someone *else*, not them. The inherent *rightness* of what he says wants to get inside me, to tell me that what he wants is the only way. It's hard to deny even though the part of me that struggles with concepts such as *right* and *wrong* is leaning hard toward *wrong*, no matter how insidiously persuasive my father can be.

That's what he's always been good at—just like any cult leader. Just like any terrorist. Taking something that makes sense, something right and true, something as simple as human rights for aberrants, and pushing it so far that you'll find yourself justifying the worst things because he makes them seem only logical. Just. Things that should be gray areas become black and white, and it's not that easy. Life isn't that easy. Life is the kind of gray area where people will justify killing a child with a toy gun just because his skin is too dark, then call the people grieving his death *rioters* and *criminals* instead of fellow humans suffering loss, pain, discrimination. The only difference between those people and aberrants is that those people chose peaceful protest when they have every right to be as violent as aberrants are, every right to take action for their rights, their lives.

But instead they talk. They fight with words, struggle to educate, refuse to be treated as second-class citizens even though other humans are just as violent toward them. Just as dismissive of their humanity as they are of ours. They've been fighting for far longer than we have. Once they, too, had to use force to claim the right to their humanity.

But they never went this far.

They never went so far as to forget that they *are* human.

Did we have to? Did *I* have to?

Sean didn't, something small in the back of my mind whispers, and I begin to tremble.

I don't have the strength to carry the weight of these thoughts. I'm a circuit on overload, on the verge of shorting out. Everything I thought I knew about myself threatens to crumble, and all it will take is one hard push from anyone in any direction to reduce me to empty fragments.

I can't face this. I can't face the broken mirror that is my father, when I'm not even sure which is the shattered reflection and which is the reality. I sink down hard on the bed, bury my face in my hand, fumble for useless words to fill a wretched and awful silence.

"Are…are you in D.C.?" I ask.

"Not anymore."

"Oh."

Just *oh*. He's killed my anger, and he knows it—but for all the wrong reasons. He's so used to having me under his spell that I doubt he realizes it's not that which keeps me quiet, but the fact that words no longer make sense, no longer have meaning when the meaning of everything has changed.

But the words he says next mean more than I can stand to think about.

"Tie up the loose ends, Spark," he commands. "Come home. I'll be sending in an airlift for extraction. Fourteen hundred hours tomorrow. Extraction point twelve."

The line goes dead, leaving me alone with nothing but Alice's mute, broken body and the soundless scream building inside the hollow cavity of my chest.

Tie up loose ends.

Loose ends.

Sean.

I don't need it spelled out when I know what he wants me to do. What I should have done in the first place. What I tried to avoid even thinking.

I have to kill the man I thought I loved.

I doubt Sean's left the city. If I were in his position, playing vigilante hero, I'd stick around to make sure my nemeses didn't try again the second I turned my back. He's still here somewhere. Watching for me. Waiting to counterattack. Waiting to keep humanity safe from monsters like me. I just have to figure out where. He's likely gone to ground in the same sort of nondescript, anonymous hole as my own hotel room. In this, he and I are just alike. Used to hiding in plain sight. University professor and student. Foreign tourist and… hm. Who would he be? What patterns would I follow, were I in his shoes?

I settle next to Alice with my laptop propped against my uninjured thigh and plug in a USB data stick, one that bounces off cell towers as far as five hundred miles out to create a ping trail so long that by the time anyone tracks it back to me, I'll be in and out and gone. And what I'm in, right now, is the MPDC city surveillance camera network, piggybacking off the wireless signal I'm riding to break into the security network. I don't bother with finesse. This isn't some fine-tuned hack job, caressing data with some thinly veiled sexual metaphor fit for a terrible nineties code-phreaker film. I'm not that talented, and the surveillance systems aren't that complicated. This is pure smash and grab. I don't care what kind of evidence I leave or who I tip off. If anyone even notices and tries to shut me out, it'll be long after I've found Sean and done what needs to be done.

And as long as I keep moving, I don't have to think about what that is.

A photo from the faculty website. A facial recognition algorithm. The footage not from the fiasco at the Capitol today, but from the airport—covering a span of twenty-four hours after he and I said goodbye in California, offset by a few hours for a cross-country flight. Right now I'm too raw to even pretend I'm not hoping I fail. I don't want to find him. I don't want to kill him. And yet here I am, doing what I'm supposed to do like a good little brainwashed soldier. Better I get to him before Jeremy or anyone worse.

There. Coming out of the gate at the airport, less than two hours after my own flight had landed. We'd just missed each other. He's just another part of a tired, harried crowd wanting nothing but to retrieve their luggage and relax, but I know the way his body moves too well. Liquid grace. Subtly understated strength. The way he glides so easily and the way his tousled hair falls over his eyes just so, until they're nothing but glimmers, like will-o'-the-wisps seen in ghostly hauntings through darkened trees.

I track him from one camera to another. Glimpses throughout the city. A taxi. A rental car pickup. Not a hotel but an apartment building, small and dingy, a decaying single-room anthill in a crime-ridden neighborhood; the camera's registration code tells me the exact block, the exact intersection. It's the kind of place that rents by the week and is easily overlooked, even if a pale Englishman stands out— especially when he emerges in a security officer's uniform, generic and stitched with the logo of a local private company.

Clever. No one looks at rent-a-cops.

I brush my fingers over the screen, tracing the little thumbnail of his face as he slips into his rented blue sedan and drives off. The lump in my throat is a *rock*, and I can't seem to swallow it. Why can't I compartmentalize this and push it away?

Why can't I tell myself it wasn't real, and empty myself of this terrible stabbing ache?

The door eases open. Instinctively, I snap the laptop closed; for my eyes only. Jeremy stands in the doorway, still wrapped in the robe. There's something at once ridiculous and menacing about the sight of an aberrant in a bathrobe, his latex-booted feet poking from under fluffy white, his hands streaked in blood and his face bruised and swollen. He looks at me with dead eyes, unreadable, as he closes the door.

"What are our orders?" he asks.

"Tie up loose ends."

"And that means?"

"You know what it means."

I stand and tuck my laptop into my bag. I'm not leaving it here with him. I don't know why I'm protecting Sean's location, but this has to be me and no other.

I dig in my bag until I find my emergency kit. Everything from adrenal stimulants to sedatives. I rip open a packet of heavy-duty painkillers. The kind soldiers use in the field to numb their bodies without dulling their minds. After swallowing the two pills dry, I sling my bag over my shoulder, check my gear, then stride quickly toward the window and the fire escape.

"Fetch your things and hers," I toss over my shoulder, clipped and quick. I don't want to be here with him any longer than I have to be, even if I'm in no hurry to assassinate my ex-lover. "Then stay with her. Medicate her to get her on her feet if you have to. Be ready to move. Extraction point twelve at fourteen hundred tomorrow. If I don't come back, go without me."

He frowns. Just a flash of disapproval and suspicion, but it says everything. "You're going alone?"

"She's out. We don't know how deep your injuries go. You may have internal bleeding as well." I yank the curtains open. "I don't need someone who's just going to hold me back."

"Are you quite certain that's the only reason?"

"Don't be tiresome."

His eyes narrow. His head tilts. "Don't be foolish, Tobias."

This standoff between us is getting closer and closer to six-shooters at high noon, and I only wonder which of us will draw first.

"I won't be," I say, then lift the window sash and duck out into the dull golden glow of a clouded late afternoon.

Chapter Sixteen

As I as ascend to the rooftops and slip across the city toward the apartment building, thunder growls and sighs. I shiver. It feels like a warning from the heavens, speaking to me in the voice of the storm. A portent. Rain is my friend. Lightning even more so. Sean may be strong, but when the storm comes down I'll be stronger.

Strong enough to kill him. Stronger than I want to be, when part of me wonders if I'm only doing this so he'll take the choice out of my hands, kill me, end this so he can live.

It's a slower journey than I'd like. Even if the pills have numbed my thigh and dulled sensation throughout my entire body, I still have to be careful on the torn muscle, gauging my swinging leaps to place my weight on my good leg and pacing myself.

More than once, too, I have to flatten myself in some shadowed crevice out of sight and wait as a helicopter or jet passes overhead. By now, in the hours since that disastrous mission, they'll have figured out we're not in the Capitol building anymore. Ports of exit throughout the city will be closed. Aerial and ground sweeps are the order of the day, likely the week. We're rats in a cage—and though I've lost the distinctive lightning-stitched coat, someone's going to notice a masked figure all in black swinging from spires and leaping across rooftops in the middle of the afternoon.

It's in one of those shadowed crevices where I conceal my bag, somewhere where I can easily fetch it on my way to the rendezvous spot. By the time I reach the back-barrio neighborhood where Sean's rented his room, the sky has clouded over into a murk that swallows the fading light of sunset. The electric prickle on the air, like lightning holding its breath, flirts with my heartbeat and tingles my flesh. I settle into a crouch on a crumbling brick building across the alley from the squat cement-block apartment building…and there he is.

Right there, past the half-broken blinds, his face cut into slats by thin bars of plastic. I'm not ready to see him. Not ready for how it knocks the wind out of me. It's like one of his cyclones got inside me, only the rush and spin are made up of all the feelings I've tried for so long to pretend I don't have.

He's sitting on the edge of a battered cot, the room otherwise empty save for some plastic takeout bags and a duffel. His mask is off, but the clinging rubber suit still sculpts every inch of him. He's tapping his fingers over a tablet PC, eyes flicking over whatever's scrolling past. Even behind his glasses, I can tell his eyes are rimmed in red.

He's been crying, and I don't have to guess why.

I close my eyes and suck in a painful breath, like swallowing nails. I have to do this. I have to do my father's will. It's the only way. The only path for me. The only thing I'm capable of. The only thing I'm *good* for. I was made for murder, and I wouldn't know how to do anything better if I tried.

I know what I have to do.

Slow and deliberate, I stand from my crouch. He stills, his head snapping up, before turning toward the window. The déjà vu is sharp and immediate. That night in the stadium. The night that started it all, when he'd noticed the *wrongness* of my body language and it drew him to me, just as it does now. Maybe we've been two polar forces this entire time, drawn to each other by opposing energy, filling each other's voids. But nothing can fill the wretched emptiness inside me when he just stares at me, that same horrible, stricken look on his face as the moment he'd realized who and what I am. It's like breaking his heart over and over again, an infinite loop that can only end in one way.

He exhales, his shoulders sagging, the color and life seeming to go out of him. Bowing his head, he tugs his glasses off, folds them neatly and methodically, and sets them aside, atop the tablet. He rises, lifts the blinds, and pushes the windowpane out on its hinges. There's nothing separating us now but the empty space across the alley. I want to say something, anything, as he steps out onto the fire escape. But I have no words.

Nor, it seems, does he, for he only shakes his head subtly and turns to climb to the next escape, and the next, and the next, flowing lithely upward to the adjacent roof before, with one last glance that borders on *come hither*, he breaks into a long, loping sprint. He's just a streak of black and white flowing across the rooftop, his hair lashing behind him in an inky banner beckoning me to follow.

He's not running from me, I realize as I vault over the edge and to the next roof, giving chase. He's leading me, like this is some odd prearranged ritual with me trailing in his wake. I know where he's taking me. *Away*, the precise location unimportant as long as it's somewhere where the clash between us won't hurt innocent civilians. It's something I've never given thought to before. It's exactly the kind of thing I'd expect *him* to think of. Collateral damage: a sign of victory for me, a sign of failure for him.

Somehow, that drives home hardest the differences between us.

Over roof and tower, across concrete and shingle, we fly: a strange funeral procession accompanied by the dirge of thunder. The sky boils as dark and harsh as the frightened thing inside me that says *stop, no, don't do this*, buried underneath fatalistic calm. Toward the outskirts of the neighborhood, he leads me — away from homes, away from people, into the derelict ruin of abandoned shipyards left to rot, just another corpse in the slaughter of the economy. It's nothing but long stretches of cracked concrete, rusted shipping containers, skeletal remains of buildings like crooked winter trees.

It's a fitting place for one of us to die.

He swings down from the roof of an empty warehouse to alight with a scuff of his boots on the far edge of a vacant lot. I'm not far behind, dropping down to ground level and catching myself in a crouch, biting back a hiss when my weak leg tries to tip me over. I can't be weak right now. Not physically, not mentally, not emotionally.

The length of the lot stretches between us, a battlefield waiting to happen, and yet I hear his voice as clearly as if he stands next to me when he speaks.

"I thought I'd have to find you."

I straighten, standing, and let the weighted end of the spool of wire on my wrist drop into my palm. "Thought I'd save you the trouble."

He's silent, looking at me, the tilt of his chin proud. No mask. I've forgotten mine, too. Here we are not Spark and the aberrant turned hero, but only Tobias and Sean, looking at each other across the field of lies and betrayal that turns everything we had into nothing.

"I'm not ready for this," he says, swallowing thickly, and

my heart cracks.

"Neither am I."

His fingers clench slowly, the creak of tightening rubber growing louder and louder. "Did you know? All this time, did you know what I was?"

"No." I shake my head. I can only be honest. Now is not the time for posturing and mockery and playing at being the villainous mastermind. There will be nothing triumphant about this. Nothing satisfactory. This grim reality demands only grim truth. "I should have. I think I was in denial."

"As was I. But I didn't want to say." Something in his eyes softens, something broken, and he takes a step toward me. "Tobias…"

I step back, bracing myself, defensive. "Don't."

Though it's not an attack I fear.

It's how vulnerable he can make me with that one soft, pleading call of my name, as if those simple syllables could change the inevitable outcome.

He stops, withdraws. Again that proud, stubborn tilt of his chin, that moment of softness vanishing even if he can't mask his grief, the lines it carves around his mouth. "This is how it has to be, then."

"It is."

The quality of the storm-born wind changes, and I know it's *him*. His will making those chill gusts whip harder, tearing at scraggly, half-dead tufts of grass and sending an empty bottle rolling across the lot with a painfully loud clatter. My fingers tighten around the weighted wire as I feel for the static prickle along my skin, the hot charge of electricity on the air, that crisp clean wildness that always surges before a storm, as if the lightning in the clouds is reaching for me, waiting for me. The silence between us is a bubble swelling to the point of bursting.

He bows his head. "As you wish, then."

There's no warning. No fanfare. Only a howl of keening wind before a wall of pure force slams into me—but I'm ready for it this time. I roll with it, throwing myself to the ground, concrete and grit scraping my bare arms as I tumble, flatten myself against the worst of it, snap my wrist out. The weighted wire goes spinning out, a darting snake striking at his ankles, snaring, tangling. I *yank* and send a hard, crackling surge down the length of the wire. He crashes to the ground with a snarl, throwing his hands up to shield his face while electricity sizzles over the protective rubber of his suit. That suit's going to be a problem—but even rubber will melt and tear apart under a concentrated lightning strike.

He kicks back, thrusts his heels against the concrete, and takes to the air, held aloft by the invisible wings of his power. I roll onto my back and wrench down hard on the wire, but he kicks it off, twisting and unraveling its coil. Suddenly the wind isn't a shearing blast, but a crushing weight slamming down on me, squeezing my lungs flat while I arch, struggling against its pinning force until my vision spins and Sean is nothing but a dark haze hovering over me, monochrome against the black field of clouds.

Clouds that light up in blinding shocks of blue and white as lightning lashes out in writhing whips, coming to heel, an obedient pet. I feel it as if it's an extension of my own body, my blood given life and surging with power, as it cracks into him from behind, dashing up against him until sparks splash off him like water as he plunges to earth and crashes roughly to the ground. The sky explodes into thunder, and the rain comes bursting down as if I've unzipped the clouds with my touch. The wind dies, the pressure rolling off me. Gasping, I roll to one knee, but he's already rising as well—shaking, smoke rising off his scorched suit, but still breathing. I tell myself I didn't hold back. I tell myself I didn't hesitate.

But if I hadn't, he'd be dead.

Rain slicks cold over my skin, gleams wet off his suit, as we watch each other breathlessly for a single frozen moment. We've crossed the line. There's no turning back. And as the moment breaks, we crash together in a violent explosion of power, of pain, of all the hurt and wrongness that it has to *be* this way. The painkillers dull the agony in my body, but it does nothing for the spikes digging deep into my heart. Deep down I wonder what it could have been like, if we really were who we'd pretended to be. If we really were just a professor and an antisocial grad student. But we aren't. We can't be.

We are the storm, and the storm is us.

He tears at me with focused blasts, lifting me high and slamming me down, flinging me up against warehouse walls and throwing me about like a rag doll while I duck, I roll, I evade with quick reflexes and lashing coils of wire that pull me free, pull him down, or leave him darting and thrown off-balance, struggling to stay out of my reach. I light him up with focused bursts of electricity, arcing from my fingers and lancing down from the clouds until he's the conduit closing the circuit between them. Over and over, breaking against each other, we strike with our powers; over and over we grapple close with gritted teeth and glaring eyes and grasping hands, only to thrust away again. Over and over we close and break apart, tearing at each other, wearing each other down, battering each other until my body is a throbbing mass of bruises and my legs don't want to hold me up, but I can't afford to stop. I can't afford to quit.

I have to kill him, in order to kill this weak and sobbing thing inside me that keeps screaming at me to stop.

Again he pummels me with a fist of concentrated wind, snapping across my upper body and sending me reeling, dizzy, tumbling to the earth. I push myself up on shaking arms as he drops unsteadily to the cracked pavement, staggering. His suit is torn, and he's bleeding—from burns, from vicious lashing lines cut by the wire. I am, too. My mouth is filled with the taste of my own blood, punched from me, cut from the inside of my cheeks. My arms are scraped, my shirt torn, a gash down my side from rolling over a shard of broken glass. My leg has torn open again, and the puddle of rainwater beneath me clouds with red. I *am* pain, but I've been conditioned to deal with pain. It's not my body that's tearing me apart.

It's the heart I'd swear I don't have.

I have to end this. Now. He takes a staggering step toward me, his lips parting, but I can't hesitate. No more holding back. No more drawing this out. It's over.

Closing my eyes, I open myself to the full force of the storm. If the brain is a neural network, then the lightning captured in the storm is an extension of my synapses. It's my blood. My breath. My life. My entire *being*, stretched out over miles of sky and gathering into a single concentrated point, building up inside me like a held breath growing tighter and tighter and more and more deliciously painful by the second. And when I let it out, when I exhale…

Night becomes day. Caged lightning roars over the lot, pouring down from the sky in a flood of white light, hissing crackles turning into a ripping explosion as it eclipses everything in a flare of sheer, raw power. It rolls over me with an almost sexual energy, trembling through me, invigorating me. I close my eyes and let it wash over me as if, if I just let myself drown in the addictive high of the surge, I won't hear the raw, ragged sound of Sean's scream beneath the fading clap of thunder.

When it fades, there's nothing but silence. I open my eyes, looking up at the sky, at the churning morass of the storm, while the rain falls down on my face and lets me pretend my burning eyes are dry and my burning heart is empty. I can't stand to look.

I can't stand to see if he's dead.

That lump is still in my throat, but it tries to claw out now in a choked sound. A sob. A fucking sob, and by the *narakas* all I want is to curl up in a ball and cry.

This tale of star-crossed lovers was never meant to end like this.

A faint groan floats over the lot. My eyes snap open. He… he's alive. He's *alive*. I don't even understand how, although humans have survived lightning strikes before; it's not the voltage that kills, but the current. I push myself up quickly and make myself look. Sean is a tumbled heap of black and white on the concrete, collapsed facedown, steam rising off him with each raindrop that pelts against him and evaporates with a hiss. But slowly he pushes his arms beneath him, dragging himself up an inch at a time, coughing and gasping and spitting out blood.

While inside, I'm torn between a sick sense of relief and an even worse sense of dread, that now I have to hurt him all over again.

Swallowing hard, I drop the weighted end of the wire into my palm and make myself approach him, each step so heavy I can barely lift my feet. As my boot scuffs against the concrete, he lifts his head. Green eyes, paled so stark they're nearly white, look up at me with pure, raw hatred. Good. He *should* hate me. I hate myself for this.

The look in his eyes challenges me. Dares me to give up my last hope of humanity, and it's a dare I have to take. I am who I am. I am what I am. I was born to be my father's son, and I'm not capable of anything else.

One last flick of my wrist. One last snap of the wire. One last wide-eyed look of realization as the deadly coil wraps around his throat, before a clench of my fist pulls it taut and it cuts into that lovely pale skin that I loved to litter with bite marks.

He gags, struggling to breathe, and clutches at the wire.

Forget powers. Forget the storm. This is human, intimate, choking the life from him one breath at a time, watching him writhe and grapple almost too quietly. There's something sick in how easy it is.

Too easy, because I can't…I can't…

His face reddens, then pales. His eyes start to roll back. All I have to do is tighten the wire, one last hard jerk, and I can't. I *can't*. My arm won't move. I can't breathe, as if I'm the one choking with the noose around my neck. My chest hurts, exploding, and I wonder for a brief second what the fuck he's doing to me before I realize he's not doing anything at all.

My heart's just breaking. Shattering apart. Crushing the careful walls of lies I built around it, exposing the red and tender thing inside — and a truth I can't bury any longer under self-deception and fear and cruelty and my father's conditioning.

I love him.

I love him and I'm killing him, and for all my fucking rationalization I can't think of a good reason *why* except that my father told me to, and like a good little puppet I obeyed.

My grip goes lax. The wire goes slack, unspooling, falling in loops around his throat. He collapses forward onto his hands, sucking in ragged, desperate breaths. I tremble, my legs cold and weak, as I step back, staring at him. Staring at this beautiful, torn, bloodied, and broken man who's stronger than I've ever realized, this wild warrior who's everything I've never known how to be. He's human. He's an aberrant. He's soft and weak and fierce and proud and perfect, and if I'd fucking killed him the human race would have lost something so special I can't stand to think of the world without him. Of a world filled with nothing but monsters like me.

And I can't stand to think of what I would have become, if I'd crossed that line and ended his life.

I drop to my knees, calves thudding painfully hard against

the concrete, and reach for him. "Sean."

He lifts his head, looking at me through haggard, weary eyes above blood-reddened lips.

Then a wall of force crashes into me, agony exploding through my battered body and dizziness rolling end over end as a blast of focused wind tumbles me across the lot.

I fetch up hard against the warehouse wall, hard enough that I hear and feel something *crack*, and I'm not sure if it's the wood or me. Groaning, I press my face into the damp cement.

I deserved that. That, and more. And he gives me *more*. A strange feeling wraps around me, like soft fingers of water, whipping air concentrated with such force that it grips me like a hand and lifts me, limp and unresisting, into the air. I know what's coming. I brace myself, but it does nothing to stop or even minimize the pain when the ground comes rushing up at me, charging with the force of a speeding train. I close my eyes right before impact, and refuse to let myself scream even when I feel every bone in my body straining to the point of breaking, twigs bent and on the verge of snapping.

Blackness tries to drag me under, bury me deep; blackness edged in the red of pain, a terrible swimming heat that pushes back the rainstorm chill. Vaguely, I hear the sound of his footsteps approaching, slow and wary. Waiting for me to fight back.

I won't.

I open my eyes. Blood films my vision, painting him in shades of crimson as he stands over me, looking down at me, his hands clenched into fists.

"Get up." His voice trembles.

I don't say anything. Don't move. I won't fight him. I won't fight the military when they respond to that flash and come running—and they will. Soon. I don't care.

I can't do this anymore.

His lips thin. "*Get up*. Fight back." When I do nothing, he lets out a broken, hurting sound and kicks me, dull pain blooming in my side. "*Get up!*"

Again that invisible hand wraps around me, swoops me up, tosses me across the lot, scours me in a layer of pain clinging to me like an acidic coating. It's fitting punishment. I'll take every lash, every bruise. His voice chases me, bitter, harsh.

"After everything you've done. All the people you've killed. You're going to lie down now, just like that? Get. *Up!*" He flings me against the warehouse wall again, drops me. "Come on. Get up. Gloat. Give me some *grand* speech about useless human morals. Aren't you enjoying this? Did you *enjoy* playing me for a fool?"

I crumple where he leaves me. He's sobbing, I realize. I'm not the only one masking my tears in the rain. He's sobbing, struggling to speak, as wretched and broken as I.

I force my eyes open and look up at him again. "No," I whisper, cracked, hoarse. "No, I didn't."

"Liar." Accusation, denial, disbelief in that one screamed word. "You lie. You *lie!* Everything you are is a lie!"

"It is." I don't know where I find it in me to smile when I can barely find the strength to even speak, but I do. I'm all right with this. I'm all right with it ending this way, as long as I don't have to kill him. "And I...I don't know what the truth is. I just...know I c-can't...can't hurt you anymore."

His eyes widen, stricken. He shakes his head. "Don't make me do this. Don't...make me be the one to end this, I...I..." He sinks to his knees next to me, his breaths gulping and shallow. "Why?"

I don't answer. I don't have an answer. Sometimes they just aren't that easy to come by.

"*Why?*" he demands again, pressing his hand to my throat, vengeance for the red-lashed marks I've left around his. I don't struggle. I don't try to choke in another breath as he presses down. "I hate you," he rasps out, his voice hitching, breaking. "I hate you for making it this way, I—I—"

Tighter that grip, and I welcome the pain, closing my eyes. Until his grasp eases off again; until his gloved fingers touch my face.

"I hate that I still love you," he growls, and kisses me.

I don't understand what's happening. I don't understand those words, or the confusing mix of emotions they rouse. But his mouth is on mine, the copper-sweet taste of his blood and my blood and rainwater and tears, hate and love and everything I crave but never deserved. He shouldn't be kissing me, but I can't tell him to stop. Not when I need this to soothe the pain and confusion inside me. Not when he's the only one who could possibly understand that I'm breaking right now. I'm breaking for him and for myself, and I only wish I'd broken years ago because, now, I'm afraid it may be too late.

His teeth, his lips, savage my mouth, punishing me with delicious pain, and I lean up into him. I'm torn to pieces, weak, and yet somehow I find the strength to wrap my arms around his shoulders, pull him atop me, fit his body to mine until his heat weighs me down in that way I know so well, that way that makes my world real again. That takes me back to those nights in his apartment, those nights in mine, those whispers of his name on my lips and the way he'd always seemed to be holding back.

There's no holding back now. No dishonesty, no lies, for all the pain between us. Everything we are has been leading to this moment. Every blow, every bruise, the accumulation of such agony and rage, clashing together until we become a force of nature building to its peak and cresting in a sudden explosive torrent of desire. We are a tangle of betrayal and confusion, of questions without answers, and the only certainties are his hands tearing at my clothing, our hips crashing together in hard bursts of friction and fire, the shock of heat and the hisses of pain each time we rake at bruises and scrapes.

Cold, gritty concrete against my naked back. Rough hands bruising my thighs, jerking them apart. Even now I fight him, grappling for dominance, forcing him over onto his back and pinning him by his shoulders with his hips gripped between my thighs and his hands digging into my waist. He looks up at me, fierce and animal in the tatters of his bodysuit, breathing roughly, his mouth swollen and bloody and so fucking perfect. I want him just like this: as battle-torn as I am, painted in the beautiful colors of violence and pain, lust and wildness, loathing and love. We're two sides of the same coin, and I can't stand turning away from him any longer.

I don't know where my jeans went. I don't care. All I know is I'm open and ready the moment his suit peels open to slide his cock against my naked flesh, burning hot against the cool slick of the rain, and I shudder as he lifts me up, taking control. For just a moment I fight him, try to break free, but his hand clamps against my throat, freezing me in place. Exerting his dominance. I don't know who's won the battle between us, but he's claimed my body with his touch, and shivering, terrible, wonderful anticipation quivers in the pit of my stomach as he lowers me down, presses his cock against me, makes me weak with the building tension rolling between us like thunder, a storm of rising need.

Then he drags me down, tears me open dry and raw with a strength no human could possess, and pain crashes over me in a vicious torrent, seeming to rip open every wound anew until I'm nothing but a living embodiment of delicious agony. I know nothing but his cock forcing deeper into me, the stretch and burn of being *filled*, and the sudden sense of satisfaction, of completion, when he sinks in to the hilt and our hips press flush together in a perfect lock as if our bodies were made to meet in just this way. I can't breathe. He won't let me, giving me not even a second to right my dizzy, spinning world before he's taking me, rolling his body in powerful flexes, lifting me up only to crash me down against him again, working his cock inside me like he wants to tear me apart from the inside out.

And I'm there with him: on fire, electric, so lost I can't stop my power from discharging in sizzling bursts that make us both cry out in pain and electroshock pleasure, static-searing friction racing over skin, heightening every sensation until every time he burns inside me I nearly scream. I'm unfettered, uncontrolled, every restraint I've ever put on myself torn free to let me just *be* in this moment, in this now. I don't care if I'm beaten half-dead, if every muscle in my body strains in whimpering protest; I throw myself into it, grinding my hips, rocking to meet him, taking every inch with a gasping desperation as if, by tearing myself apart on him, I can break the mold of what I've become and start to rebuild myself as something whole.

I claw at his chest, so completely lost, reveling in his hisses of pain and the feel of blood raking under my nails and the way tight muscles flex under my palms and ripple pale skin. He retaliates with fingers snared in my hair, dragging me down so he can bite my jaw and throat, blooming pain and burning pleasure in the touch of his lips and the roughness of his tongue. The hard edges of his teeth sink into my flesh until I whimper, go weak, the feeling running through me liquid and turning my bones to burning firewater. This is aberrant love: viciousness and desire, cruelty and sweetness, dysfunction and perfection coming together into something that's less sex and more the mad mating of two beautiful animals in heat.

And when he touches me, when he wraps his fingers around my cock and strokes me with a demand that takes control of my senses and narrows my world down to skin on skin and the roughness of his palm, the throb of blood and surging need and building madness centered on the tandem rhythm of every thrust and every caress…I lose my mind. I lose myself. I don't know the words for this, but it's somehow *pure*. Right. It's too much. It shakes me apart, and I cease to think and can only feel everything I've denied, coming out of me with the wildness of a caged thing breaking free, existing only for him.

Sean Archer. He's everything to me. I can never atone for what I've done to him. I don't know who I am without him. I'm so completely lost, and the only thing I know—as I clutch at him, as I kiss him, as I burst into a mess of blood and need and screaming-sweet sensation—is that there's no coming back from this.

Whether I live or whether I die.

Chapter Seventeen

I don't remember losing consciousness. The last thing I remember is Sean whispering, *Fuck, Tobias,* and the feeling of him spilling, wet and warm, inside me, and then everything after that is black. I don't know I've passed out until I'm waking up: slowly, at first, conscious of nothing but the red-on-black of light shining through my eyelids and the overwhelming throb of pain, as if I'm trapped inside some massive and constricting heart with its ventricles squeezing down on my body. That last memory is still with me in that scouring soreness inside, that feeling of being used and loved and taken. His name is on the tip of my tongue in a silent whisper as I open my eyes.

I stare up at an unfamiliar ceiling: washed-out, splintered beams caught in shadow, strewn with cobwebs so old even the threads of spider silk are coated in dust. The smell around me is musty and vaguely organic, like dozens of quiet bodies clustered together, and the only light comes from windows with broken-out glass, the faint sputtering yellow of streetlamps pouring through the frames. The whispered sound of rain on the rooftops is a million falling pins, the last drizzle of a storm that's mostly rained itself out.

I'm in a house, I realize. One I've never seen before. Wood-frame, abandoned, empty save for trash and broken bits of furniture and the dingy mattress I'm stretched out on. When I turn my head, something moves in my peripheral vision, and I tense.

Sean.

He sits on the floor next to the mattress, shoulders propped against the wall, one leg drawn up, his arm draped over his knee, his hair a tangle falling over his face and shoulders. I can't help a touch of grudging respect that he's even sitting upright, considering he fucked me into the pavement after the beating we gave each other. His duffel is at his side, clothes and medical supplies fountaining from it; his chest and arms are wrapped in gauze, his face patched with it.

Mine too, I realize, as I sit up with an aching wince and feel the vaguely itchy pull of bandages wrapped around my limbs, underneath a shirt that's much too big for me. His. I'm wearing his shirt, his jeans, wrapped up in the smell of him, my own clothing lost somewhere—though I've still got the wire spool clipped to my wrist, and my weapons are a dark pile of gleaming edges next to the mattress. He must have brought me here, bandaged me up, laid me to rest.

I just don't understand why.

We look at each other warily for long moments, a sense of waiting between us, before I swallow to wet my dry mouth and manage to croak out a single word.

"Hi."

He blinks, before letting out a dry, humorless chuckle. "Hi." He fishes a water bottle from his bag and offers it. "You look like hell."

"So do you." I twist the top off the bottle and swallow three greedy gulps, before forcing myself to slow down and take it with a bit more moderation, pressing my lips against the mouth of the bottle as I take another, longer look around the room. Through the windows all I can see are the edges of more dilapidated houses, swatches of potholed road, and pitted sidewalk. "Where are we?"

"East of the river. To be honest, I think this was once a trap house," he says wryly. "It's the best I could do for a temporary safe house. The armed forces were on their way. I couldn't risk my room, when no doubt your compatriots are watching it."

The thought of Jeremy and Alice fills me with revulsion, and I can't help my shudder. I don't know what's happening to me. Why I feel this way. Why I *feel* at all, but it's as if I've been drugged for the past twenty-five years and am finally starting to detox and realize just how terrible the high really made me feel.

"They're not mine," I mutter, staring down into the bottle rather than at him.

"Aren't they?" Pointed. Sharp. "What's happening here, Tobias?"

I work my jaw tightly. "You were the one who kissed me. You brought me back here. So you tell me."

"Was I supposed to leave you to die?"

"Last I checked, we were trying to kill each other."

"I don't *want* to kill you." He makes a soft, despairing sound. I look up just as he looks away, running his fingers through his hair. "But letting you live, with everything you've done, with who you *are*…"

"I know." My shoulders feel so heavy, now. Too heavy for me to hold up. "Maybe I deserve to die. I don't know anymore."

He swallows roughly. When he looks at me, those pale green eyes plead, so very lost. "How? How could you? Laos and…God, years of…*everything*."

"Because I didn't know I could do anything else." The fact

that he doesn't understand that is as confusing to me as what I've done clearly is to him, and I realize just how sheltered he's been. Either sheltered or *strong*, to be bombarded his entire life with everything thrown at aberrants and yet not become exactly what I am. "I've been told from birth that this is all I'm for. I'm still not sure... I..."

It's such a struggle to articulate, when I don't know anymore. I don't know *myself*. Not when his very existence challenges everything, and I wonder how much of who I am has been blindly accepting what I was told. No. *No*. I'm... I can't be that much of a puppet...can I?

"I could talk about the charisma of the cult leader. Brainwashing," I continue. "Conditioning. But those urges are still *mine*, Sean. The pain I enjoy inflicting on others. The inability to even *care* about the human lives I've destroyed. I feel this...vague disquiet, and that's it. If...if I wasn't broken beyond repair...wouldn't I be able to feel more than that?"

He considers me quietly, thoughtfully, pale green eyes assessing. "You've been taught your entire life that human life has no value," he murmurs. "If you want to care about their lives, you'll have to unlearn those lessons and teach yourself new ones. Teach yourself to see the world through other eyes."

"But the urges—"

"Fuck the urges!" It comes out suddenly and sharply enough to startle me into silence, staring into the snapping jade fire of his glare. His lips compress, his fingers clenching against his knee. "You think I don't have *urges*? You think I don't sometimes wake dreaming of blood dripping between my fingers? You think I haven't run from a family I love more than life itself so I won't hurt them, won't damage my very human, very fragile brother? You think I haven't laid awake at night, watching you sleep and thinking of how easy it would be to suck the very air from your lungs and leave you gasping, struggling, begging me to let you breathe?"

That darkness in his voice. That hiss, feral and low. It leaves me stunned, trembling inside, because it's the darkness inside me. It speaks to me as if we are kin, calls out to the thing inside me. Yet where my darkness keeps me on its leash, he's the one holding his darkness in a firm and collaring hand.

And I don't know how, but I can't help but admire him for it with a sharpness that makes me realize how deep this love really goes.

He takes a deep breath, smooths his hand over his knee, and leans back. "Yes. I have those thoughts. I *obsess* over those thoughts. Constantly. But that doesn't mean I have to act on them." He shakes his head. "*Humans* have those thoughts. Everyone breathing has, at some point, stopped and thought how much they'd like to hurt someone who's gotten in their way, hurt them, destroyed them, angered them, taken something they felt they deserved. We're no different." His gaze returns to me, sharp, skewering. "The only difference is how much we use what we are as an excuse."

The implied accusation rouses my pride, a flare of temper. "We were *born* this way!"

"We were born with abilities. Natural abilities. Natural differences," he flings back, firm, so convincing I almost want to believe it. "We were *taught* to be inhuman. Conditioned to think that our nature was wrong, sinful, somehow against the human condition instead of just another expression of it. Conditioned to think we cannot feel. Cannot live. Cannot love." His voice softens. "It's a lie, Tobias. It's all a lie."

"*You're* the lie!" I can't hear this. I can't hear the words that rip away the last shreds of my convictions—things that were already broken, and yet I'm clinging to the pieces because without them I'm in free fall with no idea how far down is rock bottom. "You're just an exception. An abnormality. You aren't like the rest of us."

"I am. I'm exactly like you."

"You can't be. *You can't be!* If...if you are, that means I—I—"

And suddenly, I know where rock bottom is. I know because I crash into it hard enough to crush my stomach against my spine, to stop my heart, to fill me with a realization so terrible that death would be easier than forcing these words past my numb lips.

"That means I had a choice," I whisper, and suddenly I wish he'd killed me so I wouldn't have to *look* at myself head-on and see the truth. "So many dead, and I...I had a choice."

"You did," he agrees softly. "And you have a choice now."

When I realize what he means I shake my head quickly, frantically, pushing myself back along the mattress as if physical distance can ease the sudden fear. This unmoored feeling, spinning with no direction, is terrible. Worse is this thing I think might be guilt. "I can't. I *can't*." Breathing hard, I curl up against the wall. "He's all I *have*."

"Who?"

"My father." And the only way I can choose something other than a life as Spark is to walk away from my father for good. "He's...he's my only family, and I don't...know who I am without him."

"Yes, you do." He tilts his head, watching me with a strange gentleness. "Are you afraid of him, Tobias?"

"No. I...I..." My mouth tastes like bile and sand, and I swallow, feeling as if I'm swallowing my own heart back into my chest. "I...love him. How can I love someone that monstrous?"

"The same way any son loves his father."

I hug my knees to my chest, making myself small, and I remember doing this so many times in the days after my mother died and it was just me and him—with me not knowing what to do when I knew why she was gone and it frightened me, but what frightened me even more was being alone without even the father who'd taken my mother away. That earth-shattering ache I'd felt then was the same as it is now. One night changed everything so long ago, shifted the axis of my world with a single hateful moment of silhouettes against paper screens and a single low scream and the sound of the rains. And now one night is shifting that axis again with a cruel and undeniable hand, turning everything I am on its head.

Gods…has my entire life been nothing but a desperate attempt to win the love of a murderer?

"I've…I've spent my whole life trying to be what he wanted." My eyes are burning, wet, and this time I can't blame the rain. "Because I wanted him to love me, even when he told me every day that he wasn't capable. That none of us are. And I…I became the monster he told me he was." I can't breathe. I can't breathe when suddenly everything that once made me powerful suddenly makes me a victim—yet even as a victim I'm not blameless, and I can't shake the weight of what I've done. "I don't…I don't want to be a monster anymore." I clutch a hand over the pain in my chest as if I can claw that dull, throbbing red thing out of me. "I can't keep doing this. Not for a man who will only see me as a tool, not his son."

I don't expect Sean's touch. His warmth, settling next to me; his knuckles curling against my cheek with a gentleness I don't deserve, with a tenderness I never thought I'd feel again. I've fought armies. Endured pain that would destroy most men.

But a soft touch is the one to break me and leave me curling into myself, my entire body racking with the force of the sob that tears through me as if something has reached inside, torn my soul from its seat, and twisted it into that one painful sound.

The tears I spend are a release, a catharsis, washing me empty yet never able to wash me clean. I don't know if anything can do that. I don't know if anything can save me — but at least, if I have a choice, I can choose not to damn myself further.

And the entire time, Sean holds me. While I weep, while I struggle to pull myself together, while I search inside myself for some meaning to the life I've lived and find none. I once thought the very meaning of life was its meaninglessness, but now...

Now, I wonder if that was just the lie I told myself to keep myself sane.

When I'm dry of tears, when I can breathe again, Sean strokes my hair back from my brow and guides my head to rest to his shoulder. I can hear his heart, feel it against my cheek as it rests against the soft skin of his throat, and I wonder how he can stand to touch me.

Wonder if he meant it, when he said he still loved me.

"What do you want to do?" he asks. "If you don't want to be his tool anymore."

"I don't know." Miserable, quiet, but at least it's honest. It's more honest than I've been with myself, with anyone, in a long time. "Figure out who I am without him telling me."

He smiles slightly. "That's a good start."

I don't know what to say. Like this, in his arms, I almost feel like I could be something better than what I am. If he can see me for the broken monster I've become and still stand to touch me, hold me, comfort me, love me, maybe I can start over. Find myself. Find a new way to live. Or maybe I can at least find my way to somewhere I can disappear and never hurt anyone again — even if there may be nothing I can do to stop my father from doing worse than I ever could. I can still *choose* not to break another life.

Including Sean's. I...I don't know where I'll go, what I'll do, but no matter what it is I can't put the weight of that on him. I can't put the responsibility for who I am now on my father, not wholly. And I can't put the responsibility for who I'll become on Sean. I said goodbye to him once, for all the wrong reasons.

I can do it again, for the right ones.

I make myself pull away. This one last time with him was more than I'd ever thought I'd have, and I'll hold it close to me for as long as I can—but it's time to end this. "I need to go."

He reaches for me, pale fingers stretched out. "Tobias, wait."

"Don't." I pull out of his reach, rising shakily to my feet. I'm still weak, the painkillers long absorbed into my system, but I'll manage. I tell myself my trembling is my battered body, and not how hard it is to say these words to him. To find these raw emotions I've denied and express them in inadequate words. "For what it's worth, I'm sorry. I told myself everything I felt for you was a self-serving lie, but it wasn't." It hurts to smile. That's the fucked up thing about being human. Sometimes, even things that are supposed to feel good can be nothing but pain. Like smiling. Like yearning. Like *love*. "I love you, Sean. It's the first thing I've felt since my mother died that I can be completely certain is real. But I won't ask your forgiveness. I can't."

"Even if I'm willing to give it?"

"Don't *say* that." It's too tempting, and it would be so easy to be weak enough to let him forgive me when I can't forgive myself. "Living for you is no better than living for *him*. It's just wanting your approval instead of his." I shake my head, stepping back, off the mattress, onto the splinters and dirt of the creaking floor. "I have to do this for myself."

He stands. His heart is in his eyes, and gods, he's so beautiful, so vulnerable, and I wonder how one heart can hold so much, can have room inside it to hold forgiveness for the enormity of the things I've done.

"Please—"

He stops cold. A battle-ready tension flows through him, and he lifts his head, gaze darting toward the window, searching. He holds up a hand.

"Stop."

I still midstride, poised on the balls of my feet. I can *taste* it: something wrong on the air, like the cool, razor slice of the atmosphere before a storm, that sense of something dark and dangerously powerful rolling in on an ill-blowing wind. There's a strange sound, almost *wet*, that I can't quite place although it's strangely familiar.

Disquiet rolls through me. "Do you hear—"

The wood of the walls begins to run like melting candles, liquefying into thick, waxy drips, oozing in sludgy runnels from exposed studs and wiring that begin to warp and liquefy. There's only a moment's groaning warning before the roof collapses inward in a crush of cracking, jagged beams and splintering shingles. I don't know if my reflexes save Sean or Sean's reflexes save me, but we crash into each other, diving out from beneath the falling rafters and clutching tight as we hit the ground hard and roll, tumbling over the overgrown stone paving of the front walk and skidding through the puddles of the pervasive drizzle. The house collapses in on itself in a choking cloud of dust, its groan like a last death rattle as the buckled roof settles in the sloshing pool that was once the walls.

Sean and I disentangle ourselves, pulling free and moving in near-tandem to surge breathlessly to our feet, but I know even before I stand who's waiting for us. I knew the moment that strange liquid sound tugged at my conscious memory and the walls began to melt the way wood never should.

Jeremy.

He stands in the deserted street outside the house's rickety gate, Alice at his side, her eyes so glazed and dilated she must have drugged herself on everything at hand just to get on her feet. Drugged or not, she's still dangerous. So is he, and from the way he's watching me, his lips drawn wide in an ugly, stretched sneer of pure leering pleasure, he's not here because Daddy Dearest told him to fetch the prodigal son.

"I should have known you'd get stupid." Not even pretending deference anymore. Even if he's in his costume, he's let the mask drop to show the truth behind it, and the truth fills his eyes with a hatred that's been building for years. "How very human of you. Thinking with your dick. For shame, *young Master*."

I say nothing, only considering in silence. There's a reason for this confrontation. If he'd wanted, Jeremy could have petrified or melted or vaporized us both before we knew what was happening. Alice could have drowned us from the inside with our own cerebrospinal fluid. The fact that they didn't says they're weaker than they let on. We're all battered, bruised, pretending we have the strength for this, wondering who's the closest to collapse and just how much we've got left when our reserves aren't limitless. Doing what we do takes a physical and psychological toll, as exhausting as any other. There's a reason I tap into external currents to amplify my power when I can. It leaves me less burned out, drawing less on my own internal energy to fuel my strength. It gives me more stamina.

And right now it might be my only advantage. I had the storm driving me during the fight with Sean. He may have beaten me within an inch of my life, but I've still got some reserves left. I don't want to fight, but I can.

And I will, if they make one move on Sean.

I roll my shoulders and, with a flick of my wrist, drop the weighted end of my wire into my hand, familiar and ready. "Walk away, Jeremy." Calm. I have to be calm right now. This struggle with my emotions has been clouding my judgment for longer than I care to admit, but I can't afford clouded judgment with someone like Jeremy. "Go back to my father. You want to be his little princeling, the title's yours. Take it and go."

Alice laughs—high, crazed. Definitely high off her ass. Jeremy smirks and clucks his tongue.

"Now, now. Our dearest Lord would be quite displeased with me if I let a traitor live."

"Is that all you care about? Pleasing him?"

His eyes narrow. "We weren't so different, once."

"Once." My fingers tighten on the weight. "Things change."

His upper lip curls. He flicks a glance at Sean. "You can't honestly be doing this for him."

"No," I say, and the truth of it is comfort in the moment I need it most, soothing the screaming battle tension inside me. "I'm doing this for myself."

Sean glances at me sidelong. Something passes between us. Something wordless, and yet I understand it clear as day:

I may be doing this for myself, but I'm not doing it alone.

Tattered and torn as we are…we stand together.

Meeting Jeremy's eyes unflinchingly, Sean lifts his chin. "You can't win this," he says softly.

"By what logic? You can barely stand." Jeremy's smirk turns cold. He flicks his fingers, beckoning. "Torrent, I think it's time we deposed our darling brat prince."

Before I can retort, a strange prickling feeling washes over me. My body feels strange—too hot, too tight, my skin sore and aching. A bruise-like blotch blooms on the back of my hand. Alice's little trick. My blood is boiling, expanding, capillaries already bursting.

She giggles again, a looping, strange sound. "Oh, Spark. I never thought you'd be the one to go s—"

I snap my wrist. The wire lashes out, wraps around her throat, the weighted end spiraling. She chokes. I yank back, and the pressure building inside me stops as the thin cord cuts into her neck, drawing blood—and cutting through the protective latex suit. Gagging, eyes bulging, she claws at it, but it's too late. It's reflex to unleash my power in a single sharp jolt, following deeply ingrained training that taught me to defend and counteract with a single killing stroke. It takes conscious thought to rein in the current flowing down the wire in a dazzling blaze. Alice stiffens. The stink of burning flesh rises. For a trembling moment, her body jerks and shudders. Then she collapses, unmoving.

But alive.

It's foolish, to leave her alive. Sentimental. But there's something inside me that I can't ignore, that refuses to let me murder her the same way she would have murdered me.

There's enough blood on my hands.

"Alice!" Jeremy rounds on me with a snarl. Something painful inside my chest hitches—then eases as a funneled blast of wind hits him and flings him across the street, tossing him against the sidewalk like a toy. Reeling the wire back in, I curl the weighted end in my palm. Jeremy groans, twitching and writhing, but he won't be down for long.

Sean touches my arm, a wordless gesture asking if I'm all right. If I'm ready for this. If I can work with him. A single grim nod between us answers that, and more. I want more than that touch. I want to kiss him. Claim him. Need him. Love him. I want to see that momentary flare of hope in his eyes again and again; I want him to look at me with *faith*, if only I'll take responsibility for everything I've done. I want to be the man I see reflected in his eyes. Not for his sake, but for my own. So that when I look at myself I see not a monster, but a man.

My life is my own. I can do something better.

And if Sean can be a hero, so can I.

So much in a single look. A promise to him. A promise

to myself. And for just a moment, I let myself be soft. I reach up to curl my fingers against the back of Sean's neck, drawing him close, leaning in to rest brow to brow and closing my eyes to just *feel* him, to share his breaths.

Then we pull apart as Jeremy struggles to his feet, clutching at his side. "I always knew you were weak." He spits on the pavement. "Sentimental."

I don't respond. He's tricky, and I don't have time to waste on banter. Even injured, Jeremy is dangerous—and I have to be faster if I want to live.

I draw closer, shifting the weight in my hand, judging the distance and his position, circling him. He staggers and I take my moment, whipping the weighted end of the wire toward him. He dives to the side, flinging himself to the asphalt. Something drags down on my arm, skewing my aim, and the weight skids across the ground. My shirt drips like paint— extremely dense, very heavy paint, nearly crushing me. I fling it off before it can fully liquefy. The road beneath me sinks, softening to tarry quicksand. I thrust myself back and hit the sidewalk, rolling only to come back up and whip the wire at Jeremy again. It snaps around his ankle in a narrow coil. I haul back with all my strength, wrenching him off his feet; he tumbles to the street with a snarl, starts to rise, only for Sean to fling a hand out and force him back with a gust of wind that tears past us both in an icy blast and rockets into Jeremy.

Something slices down my arm. Again—and again, thousands of needles falling from the sky, drawing narrow lines of blood. The water. He's solidified the raindrops. Sean hisses, throwing his arms up to cover himself. I fall back, hunching into my shoulders, and Jeremy laughs, echoing over the street.

"The man who destroyed Laos, cowering from a drizzle." My wire goes slack as the end of it vaporizes and dissolves. He drags himself to his feet. "That's almost cute."

My arms are slashed nearly raw, blood pouring over my skin, Sean's pale flesh a canvas of red and white. The sidewalk dissolves into a thick murk beneath us. I try to roll away, but the cuffs of my borrowed jeans have liquefied and rehardened, fused to the putty-like ground and tethering me like roots. Jeremy cackles, and it's only then that I realize how insane he truly is — and wonder if it was my father who shaped him, or if he was a lost cause long before he fell under Xinth's spell. He only needs a second more to kill us.

A second is all Sean and I need.

We work in tandem as if we've been fighting together for years. Wind sheets across the night, sluicing over us and scattering the calcified needles of water away from us in a whipping shield. I press my hand to the gooey pavement and force current through my fingers, disrupting the molecules as fast as Jeremy can change them, ionization breaking down their substance just enough for me to pull free. The thin layer of re-fused denim on the cuffs of my jeans snaps like blown glass. Both hands against the street, I let loose with a wild rip of electricity, current crackling across the puddled asphalt in spreading waves of arc lightning.

Jeremy thrusts himself backward onto the raised lip of the opposite sidewalk, breaking the connection with the damp street and throwing himself out of the way of the sizzling arcs. A focused twist of wind, blowing so hard it leaves visible tracks on the air, spears down out of the sky and spirals around him, lifting him up, but he snags onto the closest lamppost and drags himself back down, holding fast, his latex suit fluxing and warping, stretching out into ropes that bind him to the pole until not even Sean's exhausted, weakening powers can pull him loose.

"Too slow, Spark."

The air around us crystallizes. We try to shove away but hit the wall of solidified air hard enough to bounce back and crash into each other, knocking the air from my lungs. I think I feel a rib snap. Again. That'll be a matching pair for the one Sean cracked slamming me around that deserted lot. Tight needles of pain stitch up my side. I kick against the invisible barrier, but it doesn't budge.

Fuck. He's turned us into mimes in a box.

A tempest of whipping force spins inside our cage, but succeeds only in crushing us against the walls. "Sean!" I brace myself with both hands, shoving upright. "Stop!"

"Bloody hell!" Swearing, he slams a fist against a wall of solid nothingness, then winces and shakes his fist, glaring at Jeremy. "I could—"

"Not through the wall," I mutter. "You could hurt us. His barriers have a disruptive effect."

Gasping, arm clamped against his side, Jeremy disentangles himself from the light post, drops down, limps closer. "You forget. I know how you fight, and I know how to take you and your pretty little fuck toy down."

"Yeah." I flatten my hands against the air. "But I know the same about you."

Electricity surges out, tightly controlled and yet I can't stop it from prickling the fine hairs on my arms, from raising Sean's hair in a floating static cloud of living black. My power ripples along the crystallized air. Oxygen. Hydrogen. Nitrogen. It's all molecules, all atoms, all protons, neutrons, electrons.

Sean reaches for me. "Tobias—"

The right burst of electricity at the right moment and electrons rip away, atoms ionize, ions destabilize—and I'm through in a blaze of static discharge, blinding and disorienting enough that Jeremy barely has time to stumble back before I lunge into him, tackling him to the street with a strength born of pure protective rage. He can hurt me. I deserve it.

But I won't let him touch Sean.

I force Jeremy down beneath my weight. He shrieks,

his voice thin with rage. The ground quakes, swaying. The road becomes a snake, rolling and rippling in seasick waves, abandoned houses warping and running together, flowing into a tsunami of liquid matter. Streetlamps sputter out, plunging the night into moonlit shadow as they melt into the churning soup. I pin Jeremy to the rollicking street, but he grins up at me, eyes crazed.

"Kill me," he gasps, "but it won't make you human. You'll still be a monster—and you'll never be as strong as your father."

I splay my palm over his face and shove his head down. "The last thing I ever wanted to be was my father."

Every last vestige of power in me pours through his flesh. I burn like a live wire, current singing through me, dangerously bright, an electric high skimming the edge of burnout. He screams only once before the lightning lash silences him. His skin peels back, smoking and reeking, but I don't stop. Taking another life nauseates me, feels like a tally of my sins branded on my flesh, but I'll take the sin and my punishment if it means keeping Sean and anyone else safe from that mad, killing light in Jeremy's eyes.

Maybe that makes me a monster, but I need to know he's dead.

A shadow looms over me. The crushing wave of liquefied sludge surges down. I cover myself with my arms and brace. I'm going to drown—if the impact doesn't break every bone in my body first. In that last breath, that last moment, I remember the Reclining Buddha and the pink lotuses in my hand, the stems cool and the petals crisp, and tell myself I can accept this. This end to it all. The fight. The struggle. The curse of what I've done, that I can never take back. When it comes, the force hits me like a sucker punch, pummeling my body.

Not the wave.

The wind.

A hard burst swirls around me in a protective shell. Strong hands grip under my arms and lift me up, hauling me into the air and into Sean's arms. The wave crashes down over the street and washes over Jeremy's body. Over Alice's, and my gut sinks when I realize that no matter what I did, she'd died anyway. I stare down at the eddying gray muck, searching for any trace of motion, any hint that they still live.

Nothing.

There's nothing but an almost eerie stillness and, distant, the sound of sirens. It's over. Well and truly over. This clusterfuck of a mission. And, too, the life I once had. The purpose. Gone now, leaving only a simple, quiet nothingness as calming as the clean, cool silence after the rain.

My father could retaliate, burn D.C. to the ground, but not now. Anything he does now will be the petty vengeance of a petty dictator, and if I know my father, he's already cut his losses—including me. He'll retreat back to playing puppet master until his moment comes again. I can't believe he'll ever wholly let me go. I'd be a fool to think he's done with me, but that's fine.

I'm not done with him either.

Sean lowers us to the lawn where the house had been. I start to speak, but he pulls me into a tight embrace, burying his face in my hair. He's shaking. The rain pouring down is just rain again, clean and growing warm between us. I hold him close.

"I'm sorry," I whisper. "I'm so sorry. I don't know what I'm doing. I don't. But I love you. I do. I should leave, I should go, but—"

"Shh." He presses a finger to my lips. There's such pain in his eyes, and yet it still doesn't kill that spark. That spark that a week ago I would have called naive weakness and idealism, and yet I know now is his strength. "I told you, don't say it if you don't mean it. You're the one who said monsters can't love."

"Monsters can learn." And I'm willing to try. Here, broken and bloodied in his arms, twined in the wreckage we've torn each other into, I'm willing to *try*. For the first time in my life, I feel right. For the first time I know my path, and it's one of my own choosing. "I thought if I walked away, if I — but I can't. I *can't*. I've been walking away from facing responsibility for my entire life. I can't walk away from you, too."

"You really are an idiot, Tobias."

"Yeah?"

"Yeah." His eyes soften. It takes a few moments before he speaks again, voice thick. His lashes lower, and he traces his fingertips gently along the edges of a stinging, bleeding scrape along my collarbone. "Tobias, I wasn't always — " He bites his lip. "I've done some fairly terrible things of my own. I can't judge you. Not for what you've done in the past. Only for what you do in the future. Quite some time ago, I…"

He shakes his head. I wonder, now, what he must have gone through. What kind of suffering tempered him into the man he is now, and what struggles he faced to find himself beneath the stigma of the beast. He isn't pure. Isn't perfect.

But he is strong. Stubborn. Ridiculously idealistic.

And it only makes me love him more.

"That's a story for another day," I murmur. "One I hope you'll tell me."

There's a flicker of doubt. A hesitation that nearly breaks me, when it tells me the work I have to do to earn his trust. Then, faintly, he smiles. "One day." He threads his fingers into my hair and draws me closer. "One day I'll tell you everything. And one day you'll tell me. I know you and I don't know you, Tobias. Spark. But I can't make myself stop loving you, monster or not. We are all monstrous, each and every one. But you're the only monster I've ever let close enough to be able to break my heart." He makes a choked, pained sound, and yet through it all, still he smiles. "And for some reason, I want to let you do it all over again."

My throat closes. "I'd say that makes you the idiot, not me."

"Maybe I am."

His eyes are red with the aftermath of so many tears. Tears for all the people I've hurt. Tears for all the people I've killed. Tears for the people who'll be just a little bit safer, with one less aberrant determined to wipe them out. Tears for the pain I've caused him, and will continue to cause as we claw out who and what we are, and how we fit together again without the lies between us.

I want to swear I'll never give him reason to cry again, but that would be another lie. We'll destroy each other again and again, because that's what we do. It's who we are.

But in the ruin of us, we'll rebuild.

And become stronger for it, together.

He wipes at his eyes with a weak laugh. "Stop looking at me like some daft ninny and tell me you love me, you idiot. Let me hear you say it one more time."

"But it'll sound insincere if I say it now."

"*Tobias*."

I laugh when I thought I'd never be able to laugh again, but I don't say it. Words no longer matter. Nothing matters, except *showing* the man who made me human again that I love him. This is the end of a nightmare, the shattering of a thousand delusions, a cataclysm that shook my world and destroyed me to leave only that broken, stunned quiet in the wake of a disaster. Yet the shell-shocked echoes inside me demand to be filled, searching for something to light the void where my darkness and denial once resided.

What I find to wash that space clean and fill it with warmth is what I feel for Sean—this love, and the sense of freedom that comes from choosing my own fate. I draw him down and kiss him and make a promise to myself with every taste of his rainwater lips.

If I am to be a monster, I will be one both terrible and wondrous, both wrathful and righteous...and make myself worthy of his love.

Epilogue

Berkeley is still breathtaking from Lawrence Hall, even in the dead of winter. My coat does little to block the wind, but I linger anyway, watching, waiting. I'm home. This is the place I've made for myself, and no matter where the coming war takes me, this is where I'll always return. These lights are my constellations, in this man-made sky stretching to the sea.

They'll always guide me back where I belong.

When my headset beeps, I'm expecting it. I've been expecting it for weeks, but still I hesitate to answer. "Hi, Dad."

"Tobias," he responds crisply. "I suppose by now I should accept that you're not coming home."

"No. I'm not."

"You realize the position this places me in."

I know. I know all too well. I've publicly humiliated him— but worse, I've undermined his cause. Aberrants and humans worldwide now know the truth: aberrants aren't born evil. We're made that way, whether by our own beliefs or by the hatred of others. We chose a dark path for a righteous cause. I guess in that way we aren't very different from men after all.

We make mistakes trying to do what's right.

But we have a choice, and more and more are beginning to realize that. More and more have come to understand that we aren't a monolith; we're individual people with individual choices, and we don't all have to take the same path to freedom. And more and more are stepping up to take a different place in the world, and prove that we can live alongside humans. Even more, we can protect them—without losing the right to protect ourselves. To be safe. To fight for what we believe in, until we can stand as equals with humankind without having to subjugate them. We have the right to live. To be *different* without being *lesser*.

But we don't have the right to murder others to claim that.

This won't be easy. It won't be peaceful. It's that gray area again, knowing when force is necessary and when it isn't. It's having the self-control, compassion, and strength to choose the right one at the right moment when this bloody legacy still hangs over us, coloring our every action until even our right to fight for our lives is tainted by what's been done in the past—to us, by us. Humanity has never been anything but a mess of people clashing together and hurting each other for reasons that are right and wrong and somewhere in between…because what it boils down to, in the end, is that we're all afraid of each other.

Years ago, when the first aberrants emerged, they'd tried to coexist. Tried to just *be*, without forsaking their humanity— but out of fear, humanity turned against them. Made them *lesser*. Punished them for trying to claim the basic right to live. They hadn't deserved to be vilified, imprisoned, hurt the way they were. That legacy isn't our fault. We didn't choose to be hunted, branded as abnormal, monstrous, *enemy*. But the answer wasn't to slaughter all humans, though even now I'm not sure what the right choice would have been; I'm not sure what I would have done had I been there.

My father was. He was one of the first, a figurehead of the aberrant civil rights movement protesting outside the White House with a picket sign, demanding equal rights for aberrants—and standing unmoved even while humans pelted him with stones. It's a memory I'd forgotten, a truth he'd suppressed and covered over the years. He wanted to forget, I think. Sometimes shattered hope hurts less when you can forget you ever had it. I don't know what pushed him over the edge. What pushed him too far. And I want to judge him, but I can't.

Because maybe if I'd been there, if I'd faced that despair and exhaustion and the utter indifference of people who don't have to listen because it doesn't affect them, I'd have fallen over that edge, too. Maybe I still will, one day, when I'm broken by the pain of dashing my idealism against an unchanging world over and over again. I can only hope that with Sean, we can be strong enough to pull each other back from the edge as many times as we need to. Because while I won't deny other aberrants their pain, their vengeance, their rage…I can't lose myself to those things again.

And I wonder, sometimes, how often my mother watched my father's descent into darkness, tried to pull him back, and despaired when he only sank further out of her reach.

Those are the complications of war. Even when there's a clear right and wrong, both sides make choices that aren't so clear-cut when you look at the outcomes in body counts and grieving families, in failures and obstinate dogma and the pain of being shoved ten feet back for every clawed inch forward. And many of us, humans and aberrants alike, have things to atone for that not even a lifetime could repair. We're trying anyway. *I'm* trying—to repair, to rebuild. To rebuild Sean's faith in me; to rebuild a life of my own; and, one day… to rebuild Thailand, Laos, the many broken lands.

To give back what my father took.

More than anything, I'm trying to rebuild the broken pieces of self that every aberrant around the world carries inside themselves, shattered the moment they realized the world hated them just for being born. And every day, another turns against Xinth to become something better.

Something *more*.

Which makes my own father my archenemy. Some people can't change. They don't want to. I betrayed him, and for that he must destroy me.

"I'm sorry it has to be this way," I say.

"Regret is for humans. We're still better than that."

"Dad." Words on the tip of my tongue, words I need to say, but it's hard when I know he won't want to hear it. Know he won't say the same. I wonder if once he was capable of feeling these things, but time and pain burned them out of him to leave only ash. "I love you. No matter what happens. I do."

A pause. When he speaks again he sounds so old, so tired. For a moment, I hear my father again. My real father. The man who ruffled my hair and laughed when I told him about bringing orchids to the Reclining Buddha; the man who would hold me in his lap and watch the rains with a wondering smile; the man who'd been caught in an old, faded newspaper clipping with his face shining with determination, his jaw set hard with strength, his eyes trained on the White House, his sign lifted high overhead, proclaiming without doubt:

We are human too.

"I meant it when I said I missed you, son," he murmurs. "Goodbye."

The call disconnects. That's it. He's gone. And whatever spark of emotion, of a father's love, I heard for those seconds in his voice…is gone with him.

Warm arms slide around me from behind, and I lean back into Sean, closing my eyes. His fingers are gentle when he slips the earpiece from my ear and presses it into my palm. I curl my fist until the edges of the plastic bite into my flesh through the glove, and the earpiece—my last connection to Xinth, to my father—snaps. The fragments drop from my fingers. I open my eyes and watch them tumble over the edge of the roof, growing smaller and smaller as they fall.

"Are you all right?" Sean asks.

"I will be." Sighing, I turn to face him. His mask frames his eyes in darkness, until the pale green glows. The sight of him like this makes me smile. Sean Archer. Tempest, they call him on the news. I slide my hands over the warmth of his chest, the slickness of the sculpted rubber suit. "So what now, my faithful sidekick?"

He tilts his head. "We could go out for dinner, take in a film…"

I laugh. "I'm serious, Sean."

He smiles, and I know in that moment: I've made the right choice. There is no other choice for me but the one that lets me love him, need him, be human enough to want the joy and richness he brings into my life. Because I am not my father.

I am his son, and it's my legacy to set right everything he's done wrong.

"Now," Sean says, dipping down to claim my mouth, "we show mankind what heroes can do."

"No," I murmur against the perfect taste of his lips. "Now, we save the world."

Acknowledgments

Thanks to Kerri-Leigh Grady and Entangled Publishing for giving me a chance with this book. Even if most who know me as Cole McCade don't know it, this was my first published book, and one close to my heart. And thank you to Alethea and, again, to Entangled for the chance to revisit it, to make it better, to put even more of my heart into it and let it grow as a novel the same way I have as an author.

It's been a strange and interesting ride since the original publication date in 2012. I have so much love for the people I've met along the way, and for the people who've been with me all along and stuck it out this far. Thank you for being here with me. I hope you'll stay, and I hope to have the chance to repay you one day for your kindness, your warmth, and your support. There is no me without you. I write for myself; I write for you.

Together, we're everything.

About the Author

Xen is a New Orleans-born southern boy without the Southern accent, currently residing somewhere in the metropolitan wilds of Seattle. He spends his days as a suit-and-tie corporate consultant and business writer, and his nights writing — when he's not being tackled by two hyperactive cats. He also writes contemporary romance and erotica as Cole McCade, including the Crow City novels under the *Cole McCade: After Dark* erotica line. And while he spends more time than is healthy hiding in his writing cave instead of hanging around social media, you can generally find him in these usual haunts:

- Email: blackmagic@blackmagicblues.com
- Twitter: @thisblackmagic
- Facebook: https://www.facebook.com/xen.cole
- Facebook Fan Page: http://www.facebook.com/ColeMcCadeBooks
- Website & Blog: http://www.blackmagicblues.com

He's recently launched the Speak Project, an online open-access platform where anyone can anonymously or openly share or read stories of abuse — a way for survivors to overcome the silencing tactics of abusers, to speak out against what was done to them, and let other survivors know they're not alone. http://www.blackmagicblues.com/speak/

He also runs an advice column called *Dammit, Cole*, where he occasionally answers questions about everything from romance and dating to the culture of hypermasculinity, from the perspective of a male romance author: http://www.blackmagicblues.com/category/dammit-cole/

Looking for more? You can get early access to cover reveals, blurbs, contests, and other exclusives by joining the McCade's Marauders street team at: http://www.facebook.com/groups/mccadesmarauders/

Discover more Entangled Select Otherworld titles...

DIFFRACTION
an *Atrophy* novel by Jess Anastasi

Accused of being a shape-shifting alien, Commando Varean Donnelly is imprisoned onboard the Imojenna. He has abilities he keeps hidden from everyone—including the gorgeous doc examining him—because the government makes sure people as different as him disappear. For good. Doctor Kira Sasaki is determined to learn stubborn Commando Donnelly's secrets. But when she discovers who he really is, she's torn between protecting Varean or helping him escape while he still can.

DRAKON'S PROMISE
a *Blood of the Drakon* novel by N.J. Walters

Darius Varkas is a drakon. He's neither human nor dragon. He's both. He and his brothers are also the targets of an ancient order who want to capture all drakons for their blood, which can prolong a human's life. When Sarah Anderson finds a rare book belonging to the Knights of the Dragon, she's quickly thrust into a dangerous world of secrets and shifters. And when the Knights realize Sarah has a secret of her own, she becomes just as much a target as Darius. Her scary dragon shifter just might be her best chance at survival.

Unthinkable
a *Beyond Human* novel by Nina Croft

Jake Callahan, leader of the Tribe, has always believed he's one of the good guys. Now, hunted by the government he used to work for, he's taking a crash course in being bad. He's forced to kidnap scientist Christa Winters. Someone is out to obliterate the Tribe and everyone associated with it, including Christa. Only by working together to uncover the secrets behind the past, can they ever hope to have a future.

Swan Prince
a novella by Erin Lark

Trapped between his royal heritage and swan shifter status, Oliver struggles to find happiness in the life he was born to. But when he's caught in the crosshairs of a trigger-happy hunter during migration, he takes human form and seeks shelter in an old barn where he's soon discovered. Bastion's never found a naked and gorgeous man in one of his stalls before. Despite the mysterious stranger's suspicious wound, he takes Oliver in, clothes him, and nurses him back to health. When passion flares, Oliver must decide...follow his heart and stay with Bastion? Or join his flock and fulfill his royal duty?

Manufactured by Amazon.ca
Bolton, ON

14017476R00129